I had lost my psychic lock on Jennifer, and was running on my own up Palomar Mountain...

Then the roadway curved and dipped, I emerged from the shadowed terrain, and far ahead—maybe five miles ahead—shining in the moonlight, the form of a tremendous dome dominated the skyline. It could only be, and it was, the 200-inch Hale telescope, gleaming white and strangely reminiscent of a Trojan helmet.

I made a quiet arrival, without lights and at creep speed. A staff gate was wide enough for a car to pass—so I ventured inside, feeling my way along in the darkness.

Suddenly there was the big dome again, close up and even more impressive. And there was Jennifer's silver sedan parked beside it, and Jennifer, herself, struggling in the grip of two determined men who were dragging her toward another car.

Right there, in the shadow of the eye on the universe, I had myself a gun battle. I hit the ground with the Walther leading the way...

The Ashton Ford novels
By Don Pendleton

Ashes to Ashes
Eye to Eye
*Mind to Mind**

Published by
POPULAR LIBRARY   *forthcoming

DON PENDLETON

EYE TO EYE

AN ASHTON FORD NOVEL

POPULAR LIBRARY

An Imprint of Warner Books, Inc.

A Warner Communications Company

POPULAR LIBRARY EDITION

Popular Library® is a registered trademark of Warner Books, Inc.

Popular Library books are published by
Warner Books, Inc.
666 Fifth Avenue
New York, N.Y. 10103

 A Warner Communications Company

Printed in the United States of America

First Printing: August, 1986

10   9   8   7   6   5   4   3   2   1

For Ernest Holmes... wherever.
I hope he would have liked this
book. I hope he still would.

There are more things in heaven and
earth, Horatio,
Than are dreamt of in your philosophy.

—Shakespeare, *Hamlet*

CONTENTS

CHAPTER ONE
A Certain Perception

There is something about the stilled presence of a dead human body that is downright unsettling, especially if the corpse has ripened a bit and begun to decompose, because the first thing to then hit you is the odor—and it is an odor unlike anything else you may ever encounter. Once you get past the odor, a sensitive person might next be struck by the apparent incongruity of the scene—a disresonance, if you will, as though everything is out of whack here, inharmonious, something hideously wrong or evil—especially if the corpse is that of a once beautiful woman—and this perception may then well lead you into a morbid apperception that death is an unlovely and unnatural state of being.

I was experiencing all of that and more that cool December morning in Griffith Park beside the bloated corpse of Mary Ann Cunningham, a twenty-year-old coed from Pasadena, by all accounts a sweet kid with a very hopeful future in astrophysics until Death overtook her in the observatory parking lot. She had apparently been raped, strangled, and unceremoniously tossed over the wall to slide down the steep hillside

1

like so much litter, discarded when no longer needed, like an empty beer bottle or a sack of trash.

Incongruous, yes, appallingly so, and monstrous when apperception leads the mind to a realization that this beautiful, fragile package of life was callously sacrificed for a fleeting pleasure.

That was my initial reaction, anyway, and it was a rational one. We'd had a lot of these cases in Los Angeles in recent years—the so-called serial killers, sexual psychopaths, etc., who roam our streets like lobos and kill for entertainment. Mary Ann seemed the typical victim—stripped, abused, murdered, carelessly discarded. She had been missing for five days, last seen at the Griffith Park Observatory, where she worked part-time, at about noon on the preceding Monday. It had been a wet and windy day, with the observatory peak cloaked in misty clouds and occasional light rain. Mary Ann had a two o'clock class in Pasadena; she customarily left the observatory at noon on Mondays and picked up a fast-food lunch on her way to Cal Tech. Two co-workers at Griffith witnessed her exit into the parking lot bundled in plastic rain gear. She never got to the class at Cal Tech and did not return home that night. Worried parents began calling hospitals at about midnight and filed a formal police report the next morning but no police action was taken until the following Thursday when Mary Ann's car was found parked at a MacDonald's in Eagle Rock just outside Pasadena.

How did *I* get into it? Sheer accident, or so it seemed at the time. Greg Souza had called me at the ungodly hour of seven o'clock that Saturday morning and asked me to meet him at the observatory. I'd had no contact with the guy for nearly a year. We did some time together in the navy. Intelligence work. He is now a private eye, doing business in Los Angeles, and he would bring me in occasionally as a consultant. We were never exactly friends. In fact, our personalities really clash. So we sort of avoid each other, while at the same time respecting each other. And he would call me from time to time. I had managed to help him with a couple of baffling cases. I am a psychic. Or something. I don't read minds or prophesy, none of that stuff, but I do get certain insights now and then which cannot be accounted for in ordinary terms. So I am a sort of a psychic. I am also a graduate spy, and so I have learned a little about solving puzzles and developing information.

Greg Souza called me that Saturday morning and told me that he needed my help with a "terrifically important" case on which he had been working for several weeks. He had hit a dead end and was hoping that my "mental gifts" could start him along a fresh track. That is about all he told me on the telephone but I was accustomed to his tight lip and mysterious ways so I did not press for details at the moment; I just looked at the bedside clock and groaned and agreed to meet him at nine o'clock at Griffith Park.

I don't know how you feel about astronomical observatories, but I have to say that the atmosphere in these places always gives me a rush—almost a religious feeling. When you think about it, a look into deep space is really a trip to the past. These things taking shape way out there at the edge of the observable universe are really just ghostly echoes of events that took place long before the human race appeared on this planet. When the astronomer informs you that the object you are viewing is 400,000,000 light-years away, what he is really saying is that the object is so distant that it takes 400,000,000 years for the light from that object to reach the lens of the telescope—so what you are looking at through the lens could have winked out some 390,000,000 years ago, but we won't know that for another ten million years, when some lucky guy gets to "witness" the death of a galaxy which really has not existed during the life of man on earth.

I get a rush, yeah, just to be reminded of time in such big gobs and to realize that the primordial universe of some ten to twenty billion years ago can still be detected by my senses and dissected by our sciences as though the whole magnificent procession is passing right by our windows right now. Gives me a shiver, and maybe that was what set me up for Mary Ann.

This observatory is mainly a teaching facility now, except for the daily planetarium shows which are open to the public. It was nowhere near showtime and apparently there was not a lot of teaching scheduled for Saturday mornings; the place was just about deserted except for the caretakers and a few staff members. Souza was waiting for me at the check-in desk, conversing casually with a very pretty woman in designer jeans, spike-heeled boots and a lumberjack shirt, who he introduced as Jennifer Harrel and, almost in the same breath, referred to as *Dr.* Harrel—but I did not get from the introduction any amplification of the lady's identity.

She came across a bit cool but I gave her a ten on my scale anyway. With the spike heels, she was about my height. I would have called her age in the midtwenties but allowed another few years to account for that *Dr.* before her name plus a mature poise and manner. Can't say that I really liked the lady, right off. I sensed an element of condescension in her manner bordering on rudeness. Souza had introduced me as "my colleague" but she fixed her gaze on a spot several inches above my eyes and asked me, "What do you do, Mr. Ford?"

Not "how"—"what."

I muttered, "Whatever comes up," and added, with a nasty glance at Souza, "Even at seven o'clock on a Saturday morning. What's the problem here, Greg?"

He took the two of us in hand and led us several steps away from the empty desk before telling me in quietened tones why he'd awakened me at 7 A.M. It's one of the things that always bugged me about the guy. He has a basically conspiratorial mind and a flair for the dramatic, one of those guys who could make a routine weather report sound like a vital national secret: Are you cleared for this?—listen, I have it on the very best authority—I mean from an unimpeachable source—I am absolutely positive that it will be fair and warmer today.

So he pulls Jennifer Harrel and me into a tight clutch in an empty room and, in a voice probably worried about hidden microphones and/or concealed cameras, tells me, "The least I say about this for the moment, the better. I don't want to say anything to throw you off. Jennifer, listen to me. This guy is fantastic. I mean, this guy is beyond belief. The things I've seen him do..." Which was a damned lie. He hadn't seen me do a hell of a lot. "I know how you feel about this sort of thing, but what the hell..." Fine, great, he'd set me up with a hostile client. "We're at the point where we just have to say, okay, that's it, kapootie, or we have to dare to try something that some people might think of as kookie; okay, that's where we're at."

Greg Souza is five-foot seven and weighs 210 pounds. He looks like Al Pacino, overweight. But he's hard all over and a tough son of a bitch, let me tell you. Otherwise I would have hauled off and decked him, right there.

Instead, I said, mildly, "Greg, don't sell me. You've hauled my ass out of bed, now tell me why." Before he could get a word in, I said to the lady, "Don't expect Mandrake the Magician and maybe you won't be too disappointed. Let's give it a shot. What's the problem?"

She was giving me a cool appraisal as Souza told me, still barely articulating, "Like I said, I don't want to give you too much—no, belay that—I have to be honest with you, Ash—there's a lid on this thing—I *can't* give you much. Look, it's a missing person. Male, white, age seventy-two, missing since the middle of October. Walked out of this building in broad daylight and never seen again. Now, you take it. Take it from there."

Like giving a bloodhound a sniff of an old shoe and saying, "Okay, boy, go get 'im."

I said, "You know I need more than that, Greg. Did the man work here?"

The lady looked at the floor and told me in a cool, controlled voice, "'The man' is a senior astrophysicist, one of the world's best. He is largely retired but still takes on graduate students from time to time and he was doing a lecture series here at Griffith for the lay public. He has an office here. Would you like to see it?"

Souza was all smiles as she led us to a small, almost bare office in the rear. She threw the door open, almost defiantly, and stood aside while I entered. I went in and sat at the desk in a creaky swivel chair, lit a cigarette, relaxed. It was not so important that I "see" the office. I wanted the office to "see" me. And something "came" almost instantly. Understand, I have no control over these things. I command nothing, invite everything. And something came. Don't ask what it was; I don't know what it was. I just felt compelled to be up and out of there, and as I passed Dr. Harrel, I casually asked her, "Who is Mary Ann?"

She shook her head and gave me a cold reply. "Pretty good guess, there must be millions of Mary Anns, but it doesn't ring anything here."

"There is no Mary Ann, Ash," Souza said, aggrieved by my apparent strikeout.

I said, "Shut up, Greg," and pushed past him, went on along the back hallway and out a rear door onto the parking lot.

It was heavy on me—some cloistering, wriggling emotion that had my spine dancing and my eyes smarting—moving me out across the mist-enshrouded parking area and along the low rock wall, down the gently curving drive. I must have been walking quite fast; I was vaguely aware of Souza huffing along to the rear. I paused once and looked back, I guess to get my bearings, saw Jennifer Harrel following at a distance. But I could not stop and I could not wait. Something was doing me, and urgently. Let me make it quite clear: I did not know where I was going, nor why. This particular type of "psychic" activity is a form of surrender, a total surrender of the will, a willingness by the "psychic" to be influenced. I was not in a trance, and I could have killed the whole thing in an instant by simply taking back the responsibility for my own actions. I do not pretend to know the source or the nature of the influencing force. I know only that it sometimes comes to me and I sometimes accept it.

I was not trying to be cute when I said that I wanted the office to see me. I believe the thing may work both ways; the influencing force, whatever it is, may need a receptive center on which it can focus—and it may need to feel an attraction to that center. I will elaborate on that later. For now, I just want you to know that I was not in some sort of robot mode, out there on that mountaintop. I knew where I was and who I was; I just did not know where I was going, or why.

But of course you must know, by now, where I was going, and why. This is how I found the mortal remains of Mary Ann Cunningham; or, to put it another way, it is how Mary Ann found me.

I could smell her from the roadway, and I am surprised therefore that she had not already been discovered.

Greg Souza knew immediately what that odor meant.

So did Jennifer Harrel, moments later, when she joined us at the scene. "Oh my God, it's *that* Mary Ann," she moaned sickly.

I felt like crying, and I felt like hitting or kicking something, though I had never known this young lady in the bloom of her life. And I was stuck in the apperception that a death such as this is a monstrosity in a rational universe. Things simply should not happen this way, especially not now when the human mind can straddle the entire universe, not now when the ingenuity of man has allowed him to actually hear the residual echoes of the "big bang" that started it all to going... not now. This sort of death belonged to another place and time.

But then I was reminded that time and place are always relative and that the past just keeps on booming along at the speed of light, looking for a place to land. Maybe there is a planet in a neighboring galaxy where right now furry little animals are beginning to descend from trees and to walk upright—and ten million years from right now, a descendant of one of those may bend his head to a reflecting lens and marvel at the destruction of a galaxy at the edge of the universe. Then he will step outside and another descendant who for whatever reason never evolved sufficiently in his own mind to even wonder about the edge of the universe will bash him over the head, turn out his pockets for a few coins, then trash him.

"Thank God," said Greg Souza.

"Thank God for what?" I growled.

"Well, that it's not the professor."

"It's all of us," I said. "It's every damned one of us."

Souza did not get that. Jennifer Harrel did. She took my hand, and squeezed it tightly, and murmured, "Ask not for whom the bell tolls..."

It takes a certain perception, yeah, but a death like this touches us all. And the bell tolls, maybe, clear to the edge of the universe.

CHAPTER TWO
Point of View

Her beauty is not of the type that leaps across a room at you; it sort of steals over you and takes you by surprise in the close examination—a quiet beauty, deeper, more organic than cosmetic, much of it coming probably from the eyes or from behind the eyes, although the physical angles and planes are pleasingly harmonized, as well, the look of Jane Fonda or Ingrid Bergman in their prime—as opposed to, say, Jane Mansfield and Marilyn Monroe—and you feel comfortable with that kind of beauty, whatever the situation. Having said that, I guess I'm not sure I know what I mean by "comfortable"—though that word certainly describes the feeling—unless I am trying to say that Jennifer Harrel's beauty was not provocative, did not really invite subconscious seduction scenarios or other masculine tensions—which, I guess, is another way of saying that she was not sexy, which is not true, at all; she is a very sexy woman—but maybe, I guess, not at first, not right up front, her sexiness steals over you and surprises you the same way her beauty does.

Such, anyway, was the general content of my thought as

we sat across from each other in a quiet coffee shop on Los Feliz, just down the hill from the observatory.

"You're an unusual man," she'd just said to me, so I guess I was thinking that she was unusual, too.

We were both tired and cold and jangled from a long vigil on the hillside with officialdom—and probably from an over-exposure to Greg Souza, also—and I was also thinking that it was just a bit remarkable that here we were, the two of us, sharing intimate coffee after such an unpromising beginning.

Maybe she was thinking the same thing, because she quickly added, "If I seemed cool to you at first, it was probably because I very nearly detest that man."

"Why don't you fire him, then?" I asked casually.

"Can't," she replied, smiling ruefully. "Didn't hire him. But I feel obligated to cooperate. I don't have to *like* the man—hell, I'd warm his bed if that was the only way to find Isaac."

"Isaac is . . . ?"

"The missing man, yes, Isaac Donaldson. You've probably never heard of him, but anyone who ever took a course in solar physics—"

I interrupted to say, "I have, and I've heard, and I'm impressed—but I've heard nothing about his disappearance. Surely that would be worth a mention on the evening news."

She said, "Isaac was working on some secret project for the government when he disappeared. I assumed—he's so absentminded these days—I thought at first he'd just for-gotten to say good-bye to anyone and he's just sequestered somewhere on this secret project, but . . ."

"But now?" I prompted.

She raised her hands in a mystified gesture. "We can't find anyone in government who'll own up to him. And when one of my associates went to the police for information, someone very high at L.A.P.D. personally delivered the message that 'the situation' was 'federally sensitive' and that we should leave it alone."

I thought about that for a moment, then asked her, "What about his family?"

"Isaac has no family that I know of," she replied. "He was an only child. He never married. Parents died before I was born."

"You are . . . ?"

She smiled. "A friend and a disciple. I adore the man, the only one I've ever known who I would consider marrying, but I'm a couple of generations too late. He wouldn't have me, anyway." She showed me a gold band adorning her third finger, left hand. "Isaac put this ring on my finger the day I received my doctorate, as a reminder of something he'd told me while I was an undergraduate. I'd asked him why he'd never married. He told me he'd taken a lesson from the church. Priests don't marry, nuns don't marry, he said, a true scientist also should not marry because it is all the same work. If a scientist is not thoroughly absorbed by his work, he told me, then he is not a good scientist, and the work—the *work*, he said, with a capital 'W'—cannot tolerate a bad scientist."

I said, quietly, "Interesting point of view."

She twisted the ring on her finger and said, "Not only that, but it's true."

I said, "The right man maybe could change your mind about that."

She shook her head. "About marriage, maybe, but I would have to give up one for the other."

I decided to change the subject. "So who," I asked, "called in Greg Souza?"

"He's very mysterious about that," she replied, frowning and still twisting the ring. "So much so, in fact, that I first thought he was connected to the government. He didn't actually *say* so, but . . ."

I said, "It's possible. He has had federal contracts in the past."

She blinked and asked, "For what?"

I shrugged. "Greg was in Naval Intelligence. It's all one small, crazy world, the intelligence community. There are those times when it is convenient for one agency or another to farm out certain routine tasks. Greg has contacts. He gets some of the work."

Her eyes narrowed just a bit as she inquired, "How do you happen to know all this?"

I said, "I was part of that community, too, once."

She was cooling again. "He told me he had retained you as a psychic consultant."

I said, "Well, that sounds a bit more formal than the reality. I knew Greg at ONI. He—"

"What is that?"

"Office of Naval Intelligence. We were—"

"Why did you leave it?"

I held up my left hand to show her bare fingers. "Used to be a ring on this hand, an Annapolis class ring. Decided I didn't want to be married to the navy. Or to anything else, for that matter. So I . . ."

"So you do what?"

"What do you mean?"

She was still frowning. "For a living."

I said, "Oh," and waved it away.

"What does that mean?"

I smiled. "It does me."

"You're worse than Souza," she said, but with a tiny smile.

I said, "God! Then let me change the impression, quick. What do you want to know?"

"I want to know what you do for a living."

I said, "This is embarrassing."

"Why is it embarrassing?"

"Because I don't do anything for a living. Oh I do stuff,

sure, lots of stuff. But I don't do it for a living. I do it because it's interesting. And somehow, along the way, I pick up enough money to keep going."

She said, incredulous, "Don't you have any ambition?"

"For what?"

"For anything! Don't you have a goal in life? A program of some sort? A direction, at least?"

I told her, "Sure I do. I want to go on living the way I live right now. What's the connection between Mary Ann and Isaac?"

She blinked, trying to shift mental gears, and said, "What? Connection? There's no connection."

I said, "Then why did I pick her up in Isaac's office?"

She blinked again and said, "How do I know that you did?"

I told her, "Doesn't matter whether you know it or not, *I* know it, and I feel that there has to be a connection."

"Look, I'm sure you're very sincere—I mean, you probably *think* that you know what you're talking about, but..."

I said, "But it's all hogwash."

She said, "Okay, you said it, I didn't."

"Where's your scientific objectivity?" I asked her. "Can you argue with the result? I found the girl's body."

She said, "Any dog could have done that. Maybe you caught the odor."

I replied, "Any dog didn't. But let's leave it at that, it really isn't important to the question. Mary Ann was a part-time employee of the observatory. Isaac spent time there. Were they associated in any way? Did they know each other, work together, eat together—what?"

She was really agitated. "Why are you trying to link a sadistic rape-murder to the disappearance of a sweet old man? What are you trying to say?"

I guess I had become rather agitated myself, because I slapped the table with an open palm with enough force to rattle the coffee cups in their saucers and said to her, "It's all one fucking world, Jennifer! It's all tied, all connected, in some fine way! Goddamn it, you ought to know that! You're wearing the goddamn ring, I'm not! Now look at it! A man disappears and a girl dies, almost beneath the same roof and within a few weeks of each other! We call that a coincidence, damn it, only after every other question has been exhausted!"

I had made a scene. My voice, I guess, was as forceful as my open palm on the table. Not many were in that coffee shop with us, but those that were there were staring our way with open interest.

Even before I had finished my little speech, Jennifer was making her move. She scooted her chair back, dabbed at her lips with a napkin, picked up the check, and left me sitting there with spilt coffee dripping onto my lap. We had each driven our own car from the observatory. I sat there, feeling like a jerk, and watched her pay the check and leave.

The other patrons had lost interest already. The waitress came over with a sweet, understanding smile and asked if I would like more coffee. I accepted a refill, lit a cigarette, and sulked for ten minutes—trying and failing to justify the outburst to myself. She was a condescending bitch. Well, no—a bit condescending, maybe, but certainly no bitch. A typical goddamn liberated woman, probably frustrated sexually and . . . Wait, no, what are you doing, Ash—you insulted the lady, damn it, you used foul language and . . . She was baiting me, I know she was baiting me, just couldn't wait to cut me up and watch me bleed. Hey! Hey, hey, hey! What is this shit? You were a *pig*! Who was being condescending to whom? You called into question her scientific objectivity! You played mysterious mystery a la fucking Greg Souza and then you lectured her—at Ph.D., damn it, and you lectured her!—then you had to go all the way as Mr.

Macho—no, as Mr. Neanderthal—banging the damned table and splashing coffee all over the damn...

You have probably been through it yourself, in one way or another, at one time or another. So you must know how I felt. I had really begun to *like* this lady, and I guess maybe I was beginning to entertain subconscious seduction scenarios, because I was really feeling ragged about the whole thing.

Besides which, I had begun to get a feeling for Isaac Donaldson and that whole question. I had studied the man's work at Annapolis and again at war college, and I remembered how I had admired his almost mystic feeling for the natural sciences. If that man was in trouble, then... Well, hell, I needed to be involved in that. Maybe I was already involved in it, and maybe that's why I blew it with Jennifer Harrel.

I would have to give her a call, and...

Well, no, I would not have to do that. The lady was walking toward me at that very moment. She stood beside the table and, without looking at me, said, "Well are you coming or not?"

I said, quietly, "Sorry. I hadn't finished my coffee."

"Leave it," she said. "It's much better at my place."

The waitress was smiling at me.

I put a buck on the table, got up, and followed Dr. Harrel outside.

Everything, believe me, was better at her place.

CHAPTER THREE
A Compensation

I followed the good doctor in my own car, which can be pretty tricky anywhere in Southern California, but she'd taken the precaution of jotting down a Glendale address in case I "couldn't keep up"—sheer jest, no doubt, in view of the fact that she drives a Jaguar sedan while I was snorting along about two inches off her rear bumper in my impatient Maserati.

The Maserati is my chief vice. No, of course not, I cannot afford such a toy—and I will agree that no automobile ever built or dreamed of being built is worth that kind of money—but what the hell, every man has his folly: the Maserati is mine; she's my compensation for every thing I never had and never will have. Everyone should have a personal folly. So you can always say to yourself, in bad moments, "Well, maybe I'll never have a million bucks to call my own . . . but damn it, I've got my folly." Or, "Okay, she thinks I'm a jerk. But that's okay. I've got my folly." I've got mine, and she's the last thing I will ever surrender. When she's too old to run then I'll just put her up on blocks in the living room, or something, and maybe someday I'll be buried in her. Then people can say, "Well, old Ash never really made much of himself in life but, by golly, you've got to hand it to him, he'll spend eternity with his folly."

Anyway, the Maserati stayed right with the Jaguar all the way up the Glendale Freeway and into the Verdugo Mountains. I was not surprised that the lady lived in this area; made beautiful sense, with Cal Tech right next door in Pasadena, the Mt. Wilson Observatory just on up the hill along Angeles Crest, Griffith Park twenty freeway minutes away—besides which, Glendale is a beautiful community with an abundance of upper middle class neighborhoods at an altitude a bit above the normal smog belt.

I was a bit surprised, though, by the house at the end of the trek. I would not expect a young scientist to live in poverty, exactly, but I was not prepared for a hillside mansion, either, complete with electronic gate and circular drive, pool, tennis court, and still half an acre or so of lawn. Well, what the hell, I thought, people in Southern California know how to live well, that's all—for some, their home is their folly. They may eat hobo stew seven nights a week—but *God*, look at that beautiful home!

Somehow, though, I very much doubted that Jennifer Harrel ate hobo stew even once a week; just did not seem the type. I said to her, "Some crazy joint you live in."

She said to me, "Thanks. That's some crazy car you drive, too."

I shrugged and said, "Well, a Jag is only half bad."

"It has twelve cylinders," she said proudly.

I smiled and corrected myself. "One third bad, then."

She laughed delightedly—really, a very nice sound—and led me through a Venetian foyer and up two steps to the most sensual goddamned living room I have ever seen. I am talking damasks and velvets and fine oriental silks, nude sculptures in marble and bronze, coffee tables of glass and acrylics that are really *wet bars*, sectional sofa groups that could nicely accommodate several group-gropes all at once, ankle-deep pile carpeting, expensive-looking artworks everywhere. One whole wall was a curved glass bay and overlooked about 120 degrees of the Los Angeles basin, clear to the edge of the earth. A domed ceiling was about forty feet above all that. A circular steel stairway climbed gently around the walls and into the dome which was, naturally, a small observatory.

I just stood there speechless, immersed in all that, until Jennifer took my hand and led me to the window bay. Then all I could say was, "Nice, very nice."

"When the weather cooperates," she told me, "I can see Catalina. But the city lights," she added, "are really prettier under an overcast, like tonight. When it gets dark, you'll see. And remember I told you so."

It sounded as though she was planning on my staying awhile—an idea which I found not unattractive. But I stood there like a bump on the carpet and again gave my brilliant commentary: "Nice, very nice."

"Get comfortable," she said softly. "I'll go put the coffee on. Or, take a tour, if you'd like. The whole crazy joint is yours."

Didn't I wish. Well, after all, I had the Maserati. And my beach pad at Malibu, a lesser folly.

I took that tour, though—maybe only as inventory, I don't know; I think I was hung up on the sheer grandeur of this working girl's home and trying to compute income versus outgo and it simply did not compute. Mind you, I have been inside of better mansions and I have seen private art collections far more valuable than the one in this mansion. But I was recalling fragments of a conversation on a hillside in Griffith Park in which Jennifer Harrel was drawing parallels between her own struggle for an education and the one just ended for Mary Ann Cunningham, and it had been my distinct impression that Dr. Harrel was from a family of modest means; I was also recalling her story about Isaac Donaldson placing the "Bride of Science" ring on her finger—so she had not married into this. I am a certified Bachelor of Science myself, so have heard all the recruiting pitches and know somewhat about the earnings potential of scientific careers—and this "crazy joint" no way computed with that.

The master/mistress bedroom suite—(I'm no sexist)—was larger than the average family home. It was split-level. A full bath, a Jacuzzi, and a sit-down wet bar with three overstuffed backrest stools uncrowdedly shared the entry level with a walk-in closet and a vanity area to shame some cosmetics shops. The bed, capable of sleeping a basketball team, shared the lower-level window bay with a French antique desk, a projection-TV and lush sectional sofa. The same million-dollar view was available from any spot; even from the john, if you leave the door open.

The rest of the house—and there was probably another ten-thousand square feet or so—wandered away in various directions and at various levels of two to three steps up or down. There was a library and a game room and a projection room, several ordinary bedrooms, various nooks and crannies and short hallways serving as art galleries, a large formal dining room, a couple of informal dining nooks, an island gourmet kitchen with hanging brass and stainless, which is where I finished my tour just as the coffee was being readied for service.

"Still nice, very nice?" Jennifer inquired, without looking at me.

I said, "Oh yes—nice, very nice."

She laughed softly. "Surely an obvious man of the world, such as yourself, is not intimidated by opulent display."

Which gave me an excellent opportunity to be a total ass and satisfy my curiosity with some dumb question but I resisted stoutly; replying, instead, "Everything about you intimidates me, Dr. Harrel."

She gave me a soft, mocking laugh and a sparkling glance

as she carried the coffee tray past me. "Oh sure." She summoned me with a jerk of the head. "Follow me, scaredy-cat."

I followed. To the split-level bedroom. She set the coffee service on the bar, said, "Sit!—drink!"—and went on to the john.

I sat, poured a cup of coffee from the silver pot, lit a cigarette, and wondered.

You must know what I wondered.

Dr. Harrel came out of the john a moment later, switched on the Jacuzzi, pointed to it, said, "Undress!—bathe!"—then stepped into her walk-in closet.

I quit wondering, carried my coffee to the Jacuzzi and left it there while I went to the john. Then I undressed and "bathed," just as the lady ordered.

She came out of the dressing room wearing a large white bath towel like a sarong and joined me in the Jacuzzi, sat across from me, removed the towel and arranged it carefully behind her, turned back to give me a dazzling smile and a flash of luxurious boobs bobbing just beneath the surface of the agitated water, then said, "Oh damn! I forgot my coffee!"

I muttered—casually, I hope, "I'll get it"—snared a towel from a stack on the floor beside me and cinched it about my waist as I climbed out of there.

"Just black," she said, eyeing me with no trace of timidity.

I brought the whole tray over and set it beside her, removed my towel, stepped in next to her and sat down in close contact. It was electric as hell. She pointed with just a finger toward the opposite side and said, "Over there, sailor." But she said it with a smile.

I moved to my appointed spot, tasted the coffee, said, "Nice, very nice."

It cracked her up, rolled her sideways with laughter. I just sat there and grinned amiably while she got herself under control.

"You are a delightfully refreshing man, Ashton," she said, still giggling.

"So are you," I replied. "I mean, delightfully refreshing scientist."

She moved a foot onto my, uh, lap and said, "Scientists can have fun, too, can't they?"

I replied, "Not if they're married to their Work," using the capital "W" form. But I placed a foot onto her, uh, lap, too, as I continued the thought. "Would that be considered extramarital or extrascientific?"

She wiggled a couple of well-positioned toes while thinking about that, then said, "I think it would be considered just plain human. Don't you?"

I told her, "Oh, yes—say, I'm all for being human."

"Me, too," she said, with a smile and another wiggle of the toes.

I wiggled back and said, "I think human is nice, very nice."

That brought a belly laugh that kicked my foot loose. I doggedly replaced it while she settled down again enough to ask, "Human what?"

I replied, very soberly, "Oh, human anything. Sex, for example. Human sex is very nice."

"As compared to what?" she wondered, giggling.

"Well, as compared, say, to dog sex. Dogs are very locked in, very rigid, pardon the expression. The canine glans penis swells with orgasm—and, uh, you know what happens then— it's a lock. See, that would be a rather humiliating situation for humans."

She appeared to be thinking about it, then: "I don't know, Ashton. Maybe not."

"Or take the feline penis."

"Gee. Think I should?"

"Oh no, definitely not. It's barbed, see, sort of like a

harpoon. Not too bad on the downstroke but definitely little joy the other way."

"Hmmm. Is that why my kitty carries on so when she's with her boyfriend?"

"Oh I'd say so, yes. See, human is much nicer. Bovine, now, bovine is really terrible. Talk about *wham bam*. One stroke, that's all, for a bull—just one gigantic lunge, and it's *thank ya, ma'am*."

"I don't think I'd like that."

"Course not. Uh . . ."

"What?"

"If you don't mind me saying it, you give great foot."

She giggled. "Thanks. So do you. Where'd you get so smart about sex?"

"Am I?"

"You sure are. I'd never heard any of that stuff before. Is it true?"

I said, "Well, I've never done any direct research into it, but . . . I read it somewhere."

"Not at Annapolis, surely."

I said, "Possibly. You read a lot of shit at Annapolis, same as anywhere else."

"Did you learn to talk like that at Annapolis, too?"

"Talk like what?"

"You have a potty mouth."

"Oh. Sorry. I just do that when I'm nervous or upset."

"Are you nervous or upset now?"

I replied, "I think, uh, yes, I may be."

She did one of those nice laughs. "Please don't be. I promise that I will be very gentle."

I said, "Really? Oh. Well. Okay, then."

See? There *are* compensations. My life isn't *all* folly, you know.

CHAPTER FOUR
A Tilt With Candor

It turns out that the house was owned by Isaac Donaldson. He'd bought the land back in the forties, when dirt was still as cheap as dirt, and built the house many years later from a lifetime accumulation of book royalties and other unneeded earnings. Ditto, with regard to the art collection, though a substantial number of the objects came as gifts from friends and "disciples" who knew of his passion for art and could not pass up a good buy on his behalf.

And I guess the guy had a bunch of admirers. According to Jennifer Harrel, the man was practically a saint. "There is no way," she told me, "to even begin to calculate the impact Isaac has had on the advancement of science. Not so much that he's such a great scientist, though he's certainly no slouch in that department, but because he is such a tremendous person. His influence on several generations of students and young scientists is simply incalculable."

Seems that he had a habit of taking on not only the educational thirsts of young aspirants but very often their physical sustenance, as well.

"He fed the multitudes," is the way Jen put it.

Jen, yeah. We had progressed way beyond the formalities of rank even before we quit the bubbly waters of the Jacuzzi. Have you ever made love with a total stranger and noticed how easily and quickly postures and pretenses evaporate between delightfully polarized bodies? It's true. Sexual intimacy is the quickest route to absolute honesty. We should all think about that, maybe, while we take another look at our social institutions and wonder if we've gone about things all wrong. Maybe our politicians and business leaders should shake cocks instead of hands—and, you know, just don't be intimidated by all the talk of latent homosexuality; let it all hang out for awhile and see where it takes us. You know, like, "Pleased to meet you, Mrs. Jones, and what great tits you've got"— "Thank you, Mr. Smith; while you were admiring my tits, I was noticing the exciting bulge in your pants."

That's honesty, see. Cuts through all the phoney baloney and puts human relationships on a candid footing, at least. A suffering world weeps for candor.

Anyway, yes, we had progressed to first names and total intimacy then on to pet names and intimate frenzy; after all that, what's a little candor? I told Jen the whole dissolute story of my life, including the bit about being conceived on the backseat of an automobile—wherefrom came the "family name"—great-grandpappy was an admiral, you see, an Ashton of the South Carolina line; and "son of a gun" is an ancient naval term denoting illegitimate children conceived under the guns of the old sailing vessels in the days when women went down to the sea in ships as well as men, and, or course, things have always been the same between the sexes; there were a lot of sons of guns in those days. My own mother, never at a loss for wit, thought of me as a "son of the Ford" and that's the way it went on my birth certificate. Jen thought it a charming story and idly wondered how many sons of telescopes and Bunsen burners were being born in these days of sexual equality, then went totally candid and related to me her "first orgasm with a man," experienced in the shadow of the 200-inch telescope at Mt. Palomar.

"Astronomy is primarily a nighttime science, you know," she added. "And the atmosphere for sexual seduction is just darned near-perfect."

So much, I was thinking, for hallowed halls, but not for long, because her little story, I guess, stirred both of us again and we sort of abandoned everything else for another go at pure physical candor.

An hour or so later, while we lay in blissfully exhausted contemplation of the city lights spread before us like a lush carpet of sparkling jewels, Jen found the minimal articulation required to tell me about Mary Ann Cunningham. "There is a connection," she said in a whispery voice. "I didn't know her personally. Not sure I actually saw her, before today. But I knew that she came to Isaac about six months ago and told him she was dropping all her classes for awhile, maybe forever. She was pregnant. One of those chance encounter things, I take it; never saw the boy again, didn't even know his name. But she was pregnant. Couldn't face her parents with it. She was moving out of town, somewhere up north—had a job offer, I think, intended to have the baby, maybe place it for adoption, maybe raise it herself—she would decide that later.

"Isaac was fit to be tied. Had her pegged as a sure winner in the golden science sweepstakes, terribly distraught about losing her to mere motherhood. 'Any woman can have a baby,' he fussed. 'Only a few can master universal dynamics.'

"Long and short of it, he talked her into an abortion, paid for it himself, got her the job at Griffith. That's the connection, and that's all the connection. I can't recall hearing him mention her name again. Don't believe I heard it from anyone until a couple of days ago, when I heard the news that the police were investigating her disappearance. I just thought, well, maybe she met another boy and Isaac's not around to help her, *this* time. Today was only the second time I have visited Griffith myself since he's been gone. Went down there one day last month and searched his office for a clue, found nothing. No reason to go back, until today."

I asked, lazily, "You work at . . . ?"

"Sort of loosely, for Cal Tech—in research, not teaching, and—"

"What does that mean?—'sort of loosely'?"

"I'm called in on special projects. Usually at Palomar."

"That's way down toward San Diego."

"Yes. And I do consulting for JPL, and occasionally for Hughes."

"Hughes Laboratories?—up near Pepperdine Malibu?"

"Uh huh."

"Hush-hush stuff," I said.

"Yes."

"What exactly is your field?"

"Creation physics."

"You don't mean, uh . . ."

She giggled deliciously. "Not that kind of creation, no. I am trying to determine the nature of the universe before the big bang."

I was impressed, and I said so. "Nice work, very nice."

She punched me lightly in the belly and said, "I'll tell you a big secret one day if you'll stay nice, very nice."

"Why can't you tell me now?"

"Because first I have to find out how very nice you can really be."

She was not kidding, either. The candor was gone, the fun was gone, and Doctor Universe was again in the saddle. The mood was not exactly brooding—but it was certainly sober and darkly contemplative.

"Thank you for today," she said, very quietly. "I don't get many of these."

The way she said it made me think of "folly" and the human need for same. So maybe I'd had the privilege to serve as Doctor Universe's folly for the day. Which is okay enough. I'd had my tilt with total candor, too, and that was okay enough for its own sake alone.

But I found myself hoping that I would qualify, one day soon, for the beautiful doctor's "big" secret.

I could not help wondering, too, if saintly Isaac Donaldson had a secret folly somewhere which right then could be eating him alive. Or eating his corpse. And I decided that I would not rest this case until all the secrets had stepped forward and identified themselves . . . in perfect candor.

I rolled off the playing field and made my way a bit unsteadily toward the shower. Night had fallen completely and enshrouded this house on the mountain, but the glow of city lights far below and far away had found a stopping place within the window bay of the bedroom of the House of Isaac. I paused at the bathroom door and turned back to see what Dr. Jen was up to. She was softly illuminated in the glow from the window, totally absorbed with something within her own mind and totally oblivious to the lights of man.

It struck me, then, that she had not told me anything at all about her own relationship with the owner of the manse or how it worked out that she now lived there as the obvious mistress of that manse.

Do saints have mistresses?

I decided that it was none of my business and none of my concern, not even in total candor.

CHAPTER FIVE
Players

I stopped at the first pay phone along the return route and bought a call to Souza's twenty-four-hour number. I figured it was time for all the players to stand up and identify themselves, and he was first on my list. What I got, though, was Souza's "anchor," a 22-year-old named Foster Scott who wanted desperately to be a detective someday but probably never would if he stuck with the Souza Bureau of Private Investigation. Souza knows a good thing when he sees it and he knew he had the perfect anchorman in Foster Scott.

"Put Greg on, Foster," I growled.

I did not bother to identify myself because this kid never forgets a voice; furthermore, he never takes notes but can deliver verbatim an entire daylong list of messages. So I knew something was up when he failed to "recognize" me, coming back instead with a very formal, "Sorry, sir, he's mobile. But if it's important, please hang up and call right back and I'll put you on the automatic forward."

I hung up without another word, punched the number again, and this time got my man.

"I was hoping you'd call," he said, and the tone—even

considering the source—raised my hackles just a mite. "We're on radio relay so keep that in mind. What'd you get from the girl?"

Leave it to Souza to refer to a Ph.D. in creation physics as "the girl," for God's sake.

I replied, "First you tell me, pal."

"Tell you what?"

"Exactly what is going down here. Precisely who is paying your freight. Approximately what are you expecting from me."

"Can't go into that right here, old buddy."

"Then stop the goddamned car at the nearest phone booth and call me back. I'll give you the number."

"Don't know if I should do that. Think something is at my tailgate. Uh, well, maybe I better, though. We really do need to talk."

I gave him the number and had to repeat it twice. Damned guy was probably speeding along a freeway somewhere, trying to look forward and backward at the same time while also jotting a telephone number. I could picture it in my mind, and had to wonder if Ma Bell had finally reached too far in the effort to bring the world a little closer.

But I got the callback in about two minutes, and now the paranoia was unrestrained. "Listen, Ash, let's make this quick. If these guys are at state of the art, then you know as well as I do that they could have been scanning for my voiceprint and locked me in on the 'hello.' Don't go—"

"Wait, wait," I interrupted. "Which guys are these?"

"Beats hell out of me. They barged in on Foster 'bout an hour ago, flashed ID's at him. All he could make out were the screamin' eagles of some federal agency, but he says they didn't look FBI. Foster thinks the office is under surveillance right now, and so do I. I was up your way. So don't go home."

He could be the most exasperating son of a...

"Tell me about it, Greg."

"Well, you know me. Once I've seen a face, I've got it locked. Right?"

I sighed and bowed to the inevitable drama. "Right, Greg, right. You have an unbelievable mind." Amen.

"Well, I saw Hank Gavinsky tonight. Remember him?"

I did not.

"Remember?—the NSC case."

I said, "Right" just to keep him moving; didn't know what the hell he was talking about.

"Word got out just after that, maybe old Hank was doubling on us. And he flat dropped out of sight. I saw Jimmy Casaba last year during that thing with Guatemala. He told me Hank was tripling, as a double cover, and he's really a CIA hitman, now."

I said, "Greg, for God's sake . . . will you just tell me—I thought we needed to make this quick."

"Right, I'm making it as quick as I can." But the tension was building in that voice and it was even starting to infect me. "I told you I saw Hank tonight. I was out your way when Foster alerted me. So I dropped through your neighborhood, figured it was better than risking the telephones. Know where I saw Hank? Just off your driveway, pal, just parked and waiting. Don't go home tonight, Ash. Smear mud on your license plates and check into a hotel under an assumed name until I get this thing straightened out. Someone has made a terrible mistake."

I lit a cigarette, took a harsh pull at it, had to resist a very strong impulse to look over my shoulder.

Meanwhile, Souza was saying, "I know this all started with the damned TV crew."

"What damned TV crew is that, Greg?" I inquired with resignation, I know, clearly apparent in my voice.

"Out there this morning, you know, at the murder scene. That bastard got me on his Minicam, I know he did, and he probably got all of us. I saw him inside talking to the employees after you guys left, and I overheard some talk about our missing VIP. Listen, that stuff is supposed to be under the lid. It's no wonder it's blown all to hell now. The early evening news starts at four-thirty in this area. Those bastards were at my office by five-thirty."

I said, wearily, "Greg, please—what the hell are we into?"

"Not sure, old buddy, but it's plenty ripe, I can tell you that. I finally got a line on my mysterious retainer after peeling off three layers of cover. Know who we're working for?"

I said, "I can hardly wait to be told that, Greg, believe me."

"We're working for the fuckin' Russians, I think."

I said, "Oh God," and meant it as a prayer.

"That's not for sure, yet, so don't get totally unhinged. But watch your ass while I get it all straightened out. And maybe you better warn the girl."

That time I did look over my shoulder. I said, "You think . . . ?"

"Sure, it's possible. Maybe you should put her in a hotel, too. But for God's sake, don't go to the cops with this, don't go to anyone, don't trust anyone, I think we're into some deep shit here. Uh, listen, Ash . . . just in case . . . I mean, anything could happen. Right? I already gave this to Foster, just in case. Eye on the sky. Okay? Remember, eye on the sky. Now get lost."

The receiver was buzzing in my ear. I hung it up, went straight to the Maserati, turned her around, and blasted off for Verdugo Mountain. I was less than five minutes from her front door, so she'd been alone for no more than ten to twelve minutes and, besides, I had not fully bought Greg Souza's whole bag—but this guy was no dummy—a pain in the ass, maybe, but no dummy—so I had a very mixed bag of churning guts just barely under the control of a skeptical mind— not so much under control as to prevent me from liberating a Walther PPK from a trick compartment under the carpet at my feet. The long and the short of it is that I got back to the House of Isaac in three minutes flat. The hot and the cold of it is that the electronic gate was standing wide open, whereas it had closed and locked behind me just minutes earlier. A dark sedan was parked behind Jen's Jaguar in the alcove; I caught that in my peripheral vision as I stood the Maserati on her nose and bailed out running.

A skinny guy in a business suit lunged out of the sedan and rushed me. I took the angular momentum of that rush off the left hip and spun him on across the driveway and into the iron fencing. I paused briefly at the open doorway for a quick sniff of the inside atmosphere and threw a quick look over my shoulder to make sure the guy was not up and rushing again; he was not; I palmed the Walther and pushed on inside, all the guts at full wriggle now and prepared for most anything.

Greg Souza did not come by his paranoia cheaply. Let me get this explanation into the record, right here. The guy earned his spurs in the craziest of all the crazy worlds possible. The international "intelligence" community has had its good press and bad; it has been idealized, crucified, and lampooned in every media form for many years now, and the paranoid agent who sees a conspiracy in every bush is probably the most hackneyed buffoon to ever grace a television screen. I poke fun at Souza myself, even though I know with the certainty of one who has been there himself that these guys do not get that way innocently. They do live in an insane world where there is no principle or ethic and no morality larger than the mission itself. It is a world in which success is always right and failure always wrong, and there is no price that will not be paid for success.

Which is mainly why I got the hell out.

And which was why, at that moment in the House of Isaac, my guts were fairly screaming with concern for Dr. Jen.

Nor were they screaming for nothing.

This very bland-faced, pleasant looking man was on both knees beside the Jacuzzi, Jennifer was in the Jacuzzi, totally submerged, and the guy was holding her under.

He noticed my presence there just maybe a single heartbeat before I took his head in both of my hands and threw it across the wet bar. The body followed, but not exactly in a proper arc.

I did not even look for the touchdown but had the spluttering, bug-eyed beauty in my arms and hauling even before the crash beyond the bar. She was okay; a little the worse for wear but alive and well enough, which maybe was more than could be said a few minutes hence if we had hung around to discuss the matter. I wrapped her in a towel and carried her out of there, carefully placed her inside the Maserati, and away we went without a backward glance.

I thought I caught a glint of light reflecting from a metallic surface near some trees just below the drive as we flashed past that point but I was not positive I had seen anything at all, and it was no time for idle curiosity—nor was it necessary, with the Maserati beneath us. She lifted us up, up, and away—and I knew damned well that nothing on wheels behind us would so much as taste our dust until I was ready for that.

We hit the Foothill Freeway at full scream and I did not throttle-back until I'd worked us through a briskly running traffic pack and had them all numbered in my rearview.

Dr. Jen had spoken not a word and I'd had little opportunity to do more than toss her an occasional reassuring smile until that moment. But then I lit a cigarette and offered it to her. To my surprise, she accepted it and took a businesslike pull at it. So I lit another for myself and tried to wind the guts back into place.

"You okay?" I quietly inquired.

"Does mad as hell qualify?" she replied, just as quietly.

I chuckled and said, "I'd be mad, too. You looked like hell, kiddo. Snot coming out your nose, eyes all bugged and terrified. Can't you find a better way to get your kicks?"

She asked, "Did you kill him?"

I shrugged as I replied, "Unless I've lost my touch."

"How does that make you feel?"

I shrugged again. "It was his nickel. How does it make you feel?"

She did not reply to that but told me, "Ash, I'm really scared."

"We're okay for now," I assured her.

"I don't mean—I mean . . . Isaac. That man was looking for Isaac."

"He seemed pretty busy with you," I commented.

"He was trying to get me to tell him where Isaac is. I kept telling him I didn't know. And he kept pushing me back under. Why in the world would a man like that be looking for . . . ?" She made a lunge for me and held on for dear life. "My *God* but you were a beautiful sight to terrified eyes! Thank you, Ash. I don't know how to . . . just thanks, thanks."

I asked, very quietly, "Where *is* Isaac, Jen?"

"I don't know," she whispered.

I said, "I believe that you do."

"No. Please. I just don't know."

But she did. She knew.

CHAPTER SIX
The Lock

I moved from the Foothill to the Simi Valley Freeway and ran on west to Topanga Canyon then took that surface route south for roughly twenty miles to the coast, which put me down about halfway between Santa Monica and Malibu. If you are unfamiliar with the area, Topanga Canyon all the way through the Santa Monica Mountains is a tortuous course and heavily traveled, so the going was relatively slow and it was nearing eight o'clock when we hit the coast highway. Throughout that tense journey, however, we had traveled in silence, with not so much as a word between us. Which gave a lot of thinking time, and I certainly needed that. Jen needed it too, apparently—curled up beside me wearing only a damp towel, hair wetly tousled, brooding.

As we turned again westbound along the coast, she very quietly bent the silence with an almost musing observation. "What am I going to do, Ash? I'm naked. Don't even have a hairbrush, a toothbrush—nothing. I can't run around in this condition."

"The operative idea there," I suggested, "is 'run around.' You can do that. Be thankful. The other stuff is mere process.

I'll run in up here someplace and get you something to wear, cosmetics, whatever you need. Pad and pencil right in front of you. Make a list. Sizes, too, please."

She gave me a long, searching look, then sighed and went to work on her list of needs. That lasted for about twenty seconds. Then, with pencil poised above the pad and her attention apparently pointed that way, she softly inquired, "Does it bother you? That you have killed that man?"

"Maybe two of them," I corrected her, in about the same tone. "But I thought we already covered that."

She said, "No. You just shrugged it off."

I told her, "I hit a deer once. With a car. Bounded out of the darkness and froze in my headlights, not ten feet in front of me. Didn't even have time to move my foot off the accelerator before the impact. It bothered me. Yeah, it bothered me."

"Is that an allegory?"

I tossed her a smile and said, "I guess. Some things are simply unavoidable. You regret it. But you can't take it back. And there's no sense in wearing a hair shirt all your life because of it."

"But it does bother you," she decided quietly.

"If I think about it. Sure. It bothers me. Every death bothers me. It always seems wrong. Yet I know . . ."

"You and Isaac would, I believe, speak the same language."

"Glad to hear that."

"Yes. He says that death is implicit in birth, yet it always comes as a surprise; it is always resisted, always resented, and always improper . . ."

I finished the quotation, for her. "There is no such thing as a proper death."

She gave me a delighted smile. "You *have* read him."

I replied, "It has been a long time. But he keeps coming back, little by little."

Dr. Jen seemed pleased as punch about that.

I told her, "Better finish your list. Shopping center just ahead."

But her needs were simple. A few basic cosmetic items, comb and brush, sandals, jeans, pair of panties and a bra, blouse. I knew a small boutique just a few minutes from my place where all of it could be had. Took me just a couple of minutes to round it all up, then I added a small overnight bag and a simple purse to the list and used the telephone while the clerk wrote it up. Just wanted to see if anyone was home at my place. I let it ring about six times, hung up, paid for the purchase, and told the clerk a bald-faced lie. "Someone stole my friend's clothes out of the car while we were on the beach," I explained. "She's out there in the car, right now, shivering in a damp towel. Could she use your dressing room to . . . ?"

Why of course, certainly, no problem.

I left the purchase on the counter while I returned to the Maserati and told Jen, "Someone stole your clothes at the beach. There's a dressing room inside. You're welcome to use it. The stuff is paid for. Take your time. I need to check something out. Be back in ten minutes; promise."

She seemed a bit doubtful about the whole thing but gathered the towel around her, slid out of the car, and walked with surprising dignity in bare feet and towel to the shop. I escorted her to the door, kissed her forehead, and repeated, "Ten minutes."

The returning smile was a bit uncertain but she went on inside. I was in the Maserati and out of there while the clerk was showing her to the dressing room. I had no memory whatever of any "Hank Gavinsky" but I wanted to see the guy for myself if indeed he did exist and if indeed he was waiting to "see" me.

He did, and he was—well, sort of. And, yes, I recognized that face when I saw it—though probably I would not have

if we had merely bumped into each other on the street. I had
left the Maserati a block back and came up on his blind side
by foot. The car displayed a rental company decal and was
parked some fifty feet off my driveway; the window on the
driver's side was down and the radio was playing soft music
with the sound of KBIG, a popular "easy listening" L.A.
station; the guy looked half asleep.

I slid the Walther around the doorpost and nuzzled it into
his ear as I said, softly, "Bang—you're dead."

He sure was. Already. Throat cut, ear to ear. And not too
long ago. Whoever did it was either as quiet as a cat or was
able to approach as a friend: a blood-soaked sniper's pistol
equipped with silencer and scope lay in his lap; death had
indeed come, here, as a total surprise.

So much for my hastily conceived plan of action, con-
cocted during the journey through Topanga Canyon. I had
hoped to have a bit of gentle conversation with this guy—a
very candid conversation, at gunpoint—which could get directly into the heart of whichever "misunderstanding" had
sent him to my door. The only thing left of that idea now
was to elicit as much information as possible from the corpse.
But it was such a messy one, and I did not want this guy's
blood on my hands or any bloody fingerprints anywhere. I
did manage to get the coat open and to extract a slim wallet
from an inside pocket without violating the scene in any
visible way. But I learned little from the wallet, except that
Gavinsky was traveling under the identity of Walter Simonds.
He carried a Maryland driver's license and a couple of credit
cards under that name. Except for several large bills, there
was nothing else. I replaced the wallet in the inside coat-
pocket, then went to the other side of the car for a look at
the glove compartment. Car rental papers in there were under
the same name. The car had been rented at Los Angeles
International Airport. An area map, supplied by the rental
agency, had been marked with a highlighting pen to show the

route from LAX to Malibu. The car had been checked out at seven-twenty that morning. That did not compute. Why had Gavinsky marked a route from LAX to Malibu even before I was into the case? And, if his visit had nothing to do with the case of the missing scientist, then what *was* it concerned with? Why had he been sitting there just outside my door all day with a sniper's piece in his lap? Obviously the guy had been dispatched to dispatch me. But, for God's sake, why?

Ignorance can be bliss, yes. This guy had missed me by just a few minutes, probably. I had left home at about a quarter after eight, for the meeting with Souza. Gavinsky could have arrived on the scene by eight-thirty, easy, a paid assassin, settling into the wait for his pigeon with a scope and a silencer. If I had gone straight home from Griffith, I would have walked blissfully ignorant into a simple hit. But who wanted me hit? And why? On the other hand, who had hit the hitter? And why? Surely not . . . No. This was not Greg Souza's style. If he had wanted the guy out of the picture, and if he could get close enough to slit his throat, then he would have chloroformed him or hit him with some exotic state-of-the-art chemical, driven him up into the hills somewhere, torched the car and shoved it over the side. I'm not saying that Greg would *do* something like that, but that's the way he *would* do it. Greg went to the same schools that I went to.

I did some housekeeping around the scene just to make sure there was nothing of me left behind, then I got the hell away from there and took the beach way into my place, threw some things in a bag, got the hell out.

My hands were shaking so I had a problem unlocking the Maserati. I fired her up and did a quick, quiet U-turn, went on down for a few blocks, pulled over to the curb and did a quick fix on my nervous system—chemicals, yes, but from the right brain, not from any streetcorner physician. Took about forty seconds to get the rhythms into a strong alpha pattern; another twenty seconds with that focus got rid of my shakes but I came out of that feeling very agitated and disturbed about Jennifer Harrel. Nothing specific, just a hazy sort of apprehension.

I had been gone for about fifteen minutes when I nosed the Maserati into the small shopping center; for some reason, feeling more like Greg Souza every second, I did a quick recon of the parking lot, checking out the dozen or so cars that were parked there before I pulled up in front of the boutique. A couple of browsers were inside, both women, but no sign of Jennifer.

I went in, caught the clerk's attention and jerked a thumb toward the dressing room. "She still in there?"

The clerk replied, "Why, no, she left quite awhile ago."

I observed, with some irritation, "I've only been gone fifteen minutes."

The woman told me, "Well I'm sorry. She wasn't here more than five."

I said, "Look, this is serious. The lady may be suffering a bit of shock. Did she go out of here on her own steam?"

"I certainly did not kick her out, if that's what you mean," she replied huffily. "After all . . ."

I said, "No no, I'm not implying—I'm just worried about her. Did she leave here by herself?"

But I was already on this lady's list. She said, icily, "I have more to do than try to keep track of quarreling lovers. Stolen clothes, indeed."

So much for that. A small diner and a bar were the only other businesses still open in that center. I checked them both; negative. Then I saw the phone booth, out near the street, and felt drawn to it. She'd been there, in there, yes. No visible evidence, but the traces she'd left behind for me were as palpable as a perfumed scent. As I stood there, my hand on that telephone, one of the things did me and I knew I had a lock on her. It was not a voice or a vision or anything like that; I just "knew" where she'd gone, and I knew why, as though suddenly remembering something that I had done myself.

She had called "Jack," at the Hughes Laboratories, and asked to borrow a car. She had done that in a mental frenzy approaching full panic, and the subject of that panic was Isaac Donaldson. Then she had paced around that phone booth for several minutes, agitation growing, eyes flaring to identify each vehicle that turned into the shopping center. That was all I had. It was enough.

I returned to the Maserati and sent her back up the coast highway, across Malibu Creek and up the hill inland past the Pepperdine campus. The controlled-access drive leading into the Hughes complex was, yes, just a three-minute trip. Plenty enough time to dispatch a car down the hill and beat me to the shopping center. I wondered, then, however idly, if that had been about the time I was playing with my alphas.

I was parked in the shadows just below the Hughes entrance when the small silver sedan made its cautious exit and poised there for a moment before turning out onto the north-bound lane. I could not see the occupant of that car but I knew that it was her. I had a lock, so I did not even have to follow too closely.

She was heading north along Malibu Canyon Road, streaking toward the Ventura Freeway, no doubt. She would not go west from there. She would go east. I knew it, could almost feel the map spreading through her mind.

Jennifer was going to Isaac.

And so, about damn time, was I.

CHAPTER SEVEN
Eyes Up

I was running about a half-mile off Jennifer's rear bumper, surging closer for visual contact at each freeway interchange just for damn sure, as we crossed the entire Los Angeles basin from northwest to southeast—and that is a hell of a run. The Ventura Freeway merged into the Foothill at Pasadena, that one into the Corona Freeway near Pomona, streaking south by southeast from that point on Interstate 15 to join I-15E at Murietta Hot Springs—and, by now, we are rolling due south through minimally populated countryside, dairy farms and horse ranches, climbing into a high valley with the Santa Ana Mountains to the west and the San Jacinto range east—an area of beautifully sculptured "mashed potato" hillocks scattered about at random, formed as a high desert in some dim geological era but now responding to the stubborn hand of man to yield square mile upon square mile of citrus and avocado, a lush agricultural bounty which reminded me that farming remains California's number one industry.

But I was reminded, also, that I was getting deeper and deeper into backcountry while the gas gauge on the Maserati was falling faster and faster toward pure air—and this car has never been known to run on psychic energy, so I began looking for a refueling spot. I pulled off at Rancho California, a small town that has been growing steadily the past few years with the lure of country estates within commuting distance from the coast. Jennifer kept on truckin' south so I made just a quick pit-stop that give her maybe a three-to-five-mile lead. By now we are in a totally different weather situation. The air is dry and transparent, skies clear and moonlit, and I am beginning to enjoy this tour of the countryside.

I had consulted a road map during the pause at Rancho California because I really had only a very vague sensing of relative position. Best I could make it, I was about thirty miles due east of San Juan Capistrano and the Pacific, roughly fifty miles due north of San Diego on the old US395 route, now I-15, and just a few miles north of the junction with state route 76 which climbs eastward toward Palomar Mountain. I had "known" since the beginning of this trek that Palomar was our goal. I had to admit that this was probably the fastest route but if I had been setting off on my own I would undoubtedly have taken the coast route to Oceanside then SR76 into the interior.

As it worked out, I found myself "on my own" very shortly after the refueling stop. I didn't understand what was happening, at first; it just seemed that my "lock" with Jennifer was weakening. Yet I knew from past experience that this could not be the result of distancing. Distance apparently has no effect on psychic energy; I can leap to London or Paris at the speed of light, in my mind, and so can you. A mere four or five terrestrial miles of separation between attuned minds would not affect that linkage.

Yet I was losing her and I knew it. Let me see if I can explain that, to at least some approximation of ordinary experience. If you have ever had your car radio tuned to an FM broadcast while driving cross-country, you have probably noticed a "fringe area" at the outermost range of a particular station, an area in which the broadcast volume begins to subside or to waver, sometimes gaining strength again as you climb to a higher elevation, sometimes disappearing altogether–and sometimes you may experience a Ping-Pong effect between two stations at the same wavelength, where first you hear one station and then the other, back and forth like that until you finally leave one station's influence altogether and your radio "locks on" to the other.

That is sort of like the problem I was having with Jennifer. I was losing the "lock"—but unlike radio waves, which are affected by distancing, my "mental wavelength" should have an infinite range, so I could not understand why I was having the problem. At first. I could only presume that she had turned east onto the little two-lane state highway 76 toward the Pala Indian reservation and Palomar, since she had blinked-out on me and I was strictly on my own at that point.

I was forced to consciously break the energy link as I approached the tiny village of Pala, which is within the reservation. "Forced" the same way you may be forced to turn off your radio during an electrical storm: the background noise simply becomes so loud and disturbing that you cannot tolerate it.

This was not my first encounter with an Indian reservation. I had experienced disturbing "hits" before in the vicinity of Indian holy grounds but never anything like this. For lack of a better explanation, at the time, I decided that the interference could be the result of special properties of this particular Indian area, and I made a mental note to look into that closer one day.

At any rate, I lost my lock on Jennifer and I did not get it back. Don't ever bet your life on a psychic's infallibility— and do not ever trust any psychic who claims to be one hundred percent all of the time. The thing simply does not work that way. We do not command it. It commands us, and we can only humbly respond; start feeling arrogant about "the power" and you lose it damned quick. Keep that in mind during your own tentative explorations into psychism, and particularly keep it in mind when consulting any self-proclaimed "psychic."

So—I was running on my own, at night, in unfamiliar country, when I began the ascent up Palomar Mountain, over six-thousand feet to the peak, from near sea level—a winding and twisting two-lane blacktop with numerous switchbacks. Moreover, I began to note patches of snow as the climb continued, then banked snow along the edges of the road, and icy spots on the roadway itself. So there was really no thought toward any attempt to overtake Jennifer; I was simply trusting the earlier reading that Palomar was the destination, while taking great care that the Maserati make it all the way without incident.

I did not encounter a single vehicle along the way from the moment I left the state highway and began the climb along the country road up the mountain, nor were there any signs of life whatever until I hit the national park area at the five-thousand-foot level. At that point, a small rustic complex housed a cafe and market, both closed for the night, and a roadway signboard informed me that I was still six miles from the observatory. I pulled into the parking area and lit a cigarette, got out of the car and stretched my legs, wondering what the hell I was going to do when I reached the end of the road; I had given no thought to that, had never been to Palomar before, really knew nothing about the place.

I did know that Cal Tech (the California Institute of Technology) owned the facility, and I recalled reading something to the effect that the Carnegie Institution shared administrative responsibilities and had something to do with research priorities. The 200-inch Hale telescope which had been installed there during the 1940s had been the world's largest optical instrument until just recently, when the Russians completed a 236-inch reflector; Palomar, though, continued to be the free world's chief "eye on the heavens," capable of "seeing" to the edge of the known universe, more than one billion light-years distant.

So much for that, what I knew about Palomar. I had no idea whatever of the layout of the physical facility. Accessibility, security . . . none of that.

While I was stretching my legs and wondering about things like that, a woman came out of the market and locked the door from the outside, looked at me, at my car, back at me again in some quick sizing-up, then called over to me, "Sorry, we're closed."

I replied, "Yes, thanks, I noticed your sign. Just stretching the legs."

She observed, amiably, "Cold tonight."

I said, "Sure is."

She continued to stand at the door, watching me with probably more curiosity than anything else. "Observatory is straight ahead," she informed me.

I said, "Thanks. I was following Dr. Harrel. Guess I got a little behind. Lots of ice, back there. Be careful, if you're heading that way."

"Oh no, I live on up the road," she replied. "A car went by just a couple of minutes ahead of you, so you're not far behind." She was moving toward the far side of the building; I presumed she had a car parked back there somewhere.

I called after her, "People actually live up here?"

She laughed as she returned that one and disappeared around the corner. "More than you'd think."

More than anyone would think, yes. I could not remember when I had felt more isolated from the rest of humanity. The silence seemed absolute, pure and pristine, and the darkness unmarred by human presence. Which, I guess, is why this mountaintop was chosen as the site for the eye on the universe.

Twice in recent moments, the "eye" thing had streaked my reflective processes. And I thought, then, of the last thing said to me by Greg Souza, just as the real nuttiness was beginning: "... just in case, eye on the sky. Remember, eye on the sky."

Which, I had thought at the moment, meant not a hell of a lot in this present arena. Every observatory was an "eye on the sky" and every astronomer had one. Unless, I was now thinking, "eye on the sky" was a code phrase for some sort of operation involving the disappearance of Isaac Donaldson, some sort of *intelligence* operation. There was no mistaking the implication that Souza was providing a clue to his own death or disappearance, should either occur—a pointer of some kind toward those responsible.

Whatever, I could not help thinking that this mountaintop, so perfect for an eye on the sky, was also a perfect setting for skulduggery.

It is, as the crow flies, no more than thirty miles from the sea, fifty miles from the heart of San Diego, a hundred miles from the L.A. Civic Center—yet isolated in primitive splendor, a remote island of almost pure nature arising at the edge of the greatest population density west of New York City.

I was enveloped in the feeling that only the Maserati and I were afloat in this world, immersed in the dark silence which was broken only by the hum of a well-tuned engine and the well-defined cone of light from the headlamps, an almost vertigo-like feeling as I went on toward the unseen peak of the mountain. But all of that changed in an instant; the roadway curved and dipped, the horizon instantly elevated beyond screening trees as I emerged from the shadowed terrain, and far ahead—maybe five miles ahead—shining in the moonlight, the hand of man reappeared in the form of a tremendous dome dominating the skyline. It could only be, and it was, the 200-inch Hale telescope, gleaming white in the light of the moon and strangely reminiscent of a Trojan helmet.

I am going to give you here some facts I later looked up

regarding this astonishing structure. A telescope is sized by
the diameter of its reflector; 200 inches or seventeen feet is
the diameter of the tube itself, which is also sixty feet long.
The main mirror weighs fourteen tons, the entire moveable
assembly more than 500 tons, yet all balanced and supported
so smoothly that a 1/12-hp motor can turn it. This entire
apparatus is enclosed within the dome; the entire "building,"
then, moves along an east-west axis while the telescopic
barrel, inside the dome, moves on a north-south axis.

It is an impressive sight, especially in that first glimpse
and in context with the setting; I was certainly impressed. I
stopped the car again and sat there for several seconds just
sort of getting the lay of the land and the feel of the moment.
The shutters of the dome were closed. They are emplaced
vertically, of course, to accommodate the north-south align-
ment, and are responsible for the Trojan helmet appearance.
Closed shutters meant, I presumed, no activity inside; and,
indeed, at that distance, I could discern no evidence of any
activity whatever on that peak.

I decided on a quiet arrival, making the final approach
without lights and at creep speed. The periphery was fenced—
chainlink topped with barbed wire—and appropriately identified as Cal-Tech property. The place is open to the public
during the day but now the visitors' gate was closed and
locked. Another gate, obviously for staff use, was unlocked
and partially open—just wide enough for a car to pass—so
I ventured on inside.

Actually the big dome is one of five domes at Palomar,
ranging from an eighteen-inch up to the big one, scattered
about the mountaintop over a fairly wide area. I had no idea
how much area was actually involved nor how many build-
ings, residences, etc., were there. So I was really on uncertain
ground and simply feeling my way along in the darkness,
now and then in open moonlight but mostly in deep shadows.

All that changed, though, as suddenly and dramatically as

that first glimpse of the big dome. Suddenly there it was again, bathed by the moon—immense, in the closeup, and even more impressive. And there was Jennifer's borrowed silver sedan, parked beside it, and there was Jennifer, herself, struggling in the grip of two determined men who were dragging her toward another car—and, off to one side, there was my old pal Greg Souza, just a casual observer.

I hit the ground with the Walther leading the way, even before the thinking part of me could assimilate all that, and I fired a shot "across the bow" to announce a new element in the drama. Actually I sent the round into that other vehicle. Both guys reacted to that by releasing Jennifer and clawing for their own weapons.

So . . . shit. Right there in the shadow of the eye on the universe, I had myself a gun battle.

CHAPTER EIGHT
Incident at Palomar

No more than a dozen shots were fired, in all—four of them mine. I was going not for a kill but for a statement, that being: you can't have her all that easy, guys. Keep in mind that I did not yet know the name of the game nor even the identities of the players. Hell, these guys could be FBI, local police, anything. So it's nice, at such a time, to be a marksman. My general theory of firearms, in fact, is that anyone who owns one should take the time to thoroughly understand ballistics science and to master the art of sending a bullet to a precise mark. So I am a marksman and I sent four to carefully selected targets; the first, to capture attention; the others, to encourage sane thought. I grazed both of those guys in nonvital areas—an arm of one, a leg of another—deep enough to etch a pretty good groove and produce some bleeding. Meanwhile, their return fire was totally ineffective, mainly because they could not see me. I was in dark shadow while they were brightly illuminated by the headlights of their own car. So they got very sane, very quickly, and got the hell out of there—a bullet-hole in their door and a lot of pain behind the wheel, if the erratic course of that fleeing vehicle was any measure. That reaction answered at least one identity question as well. I have never known cops to run away from a fight; they just hunker down and wait for help, if that is needed.

Jennifer had run inside the building the instant she was released. Souza was standing exactly where I had first seen him, hands raised over his head and peering into the darkness from which my first round had erupted. "I am not armed," he announced to the world at large in a calm voice.

I called back, "You should be, you asshole."

The arms came down immediately and he replied with obvious relief, "That you, Ash?"

I said, "Yeh," and joined him in the moonlight.

"You should have iced those bastards," he told me.

"Who are they?"

"Beats me. You're the one was throwing lead at them. I figured you knew."

I told him, "This thing is getting crazy. Or I guess you know that already. Nice work you did on Gavinsky."

He said, "Thanks"—then did a double take with: "What's that nice work I did?"

"You didn't do it?"

"Damned if I know, Ash. What're we talking about?"

"I went home," I explained. "Gavinsky was still there. Well . . . his body was. Someone did his throat. Ear to ear."

Souza winced, said, "No, don't credit me with that. You're right, it's getting crazier. Look. We need to talk."

"Right now," I replied, "I need some words with Dr. Harrel."

"She ran inside."

I said, "Yeah, I noticed. What the hell are you doing here, Greg?"

"Just came down to look it over," he told me. "Been here a couple of hours. Surprised as hell to see the girl come streaking in here. God, she looked wild. Saw me and started running. Right into the arms of these other jerks. I don't know what the hell . . ."

I was looking at her car, the way it was parked beside the observatory. "She didn't come in the way I did," I observed.

"First time she did," Souza said thoughtfully. "If you mean straight in from the front gate. But she turned off and went over toward the offices. Didn't know it was her, then, but she came back like shot out of hell, jumped out of the car almost before it quit rolling. I thought—"

I interrupted with, "Later, Greg—stay right here," and I went quickly inside to find the lady. She was probably scared half to death, I was thinking, and needed to know that the situation was in hand—for the moment, anyway.

But I did not find the lady inside there. I found a guy in blue jeans and checkered shirt, tiny round eyeglasses and bird's-nest beard—about my age, very nervous, wary of me— emerging from an elevator which, I presumed, served as the chief route to the interior of the massive structure.

He asked me, "Were those gunshots?"

I told him, "You bet they were. Where did Jennifer go?"

He said, "Jennifer who?"

I said, "Jennifer Harrel. She was accosted just outside by a couple of weirdos. She ran in here."

He said, "I don't know Jennifer Harrel, except by reputation. I was up in the cage. If she came in here . . . I don't know. Who are you?"

"Security," I lied. "She must be inside somewhere."

The guy seemed to have bought the "security" gag. His attitude became much more relaxed and a lot more helpful. "If we start getting creeps up here . . ." He was holding the elevator door open, ushering me inside.

"Why were you in the cage?" I asked him conversationally. "I noticed the shutters are closed."

"Moonset pretty soon, now," he replied. "We'll have a nice dark sky; I was just getting ready." He showed me a delighted, boyish grin. "I get ten minutes of direct observation, from the cage." This, with all the enthusiasm of a ten-year-old's announcement of a trip to the circus.

"Not much of that, anymore," I ventured, not knowing what the hell I was talking about.

"Well, it's pretty inefficient, and there's just so much observing time to go around. But I really love to touch the universe as directly as possible. The control room is more comfortable, sure, but . . ."

A true astronomer, this one, filled with the romance of it all; a poet in scientific garb. The "cage," I recalled from something Jennifer had told me, is a six-foot capsule near the upper end of the telescope in which the astronomer "rides" and carries on his/her observations. It could get very cold and intensely uncomfortable. At one time, here, it was the only way. Now the whole thing was accomplished from the comfort of armchairs in a heated, well-lit control room, with a computer and video screens. But that "cage" had figured rather prominently in the stirring little seduction story Jennifer shared with me—love among the stars, okay.

But there was no "love" in there tonight . . . just instrument panels and gadgets, video screens, a couple of weary looking guys in blue jeans going through some calculations on the computer. Jennifer was not in there.

"You might try the catwalk," the poet suggested, indicating a door behind me.

I went out there—or in there, whatever—and was immediately swallowed by an immensity of steel girders and whatnot, the support structure for this mammoth eye. There was not a sound or a movement out there beneath the dome—but I thought I detected a door slightly ajar on the other side. I went down there to check it out, discovered a door was indeed ajar and that it led to the visitors' gallery. I went on through, down a long, winding flight of stairs, and found myself outside on the building's far side.

So, what the hell, I followed a sidewalk around the building and rejoined Souza. He was seated in his car with a door open, shivering slightly in the chill air, chatting with a couple of guys who were seated in a car idling with lights off beside his.

As I moved between the two vehicles, Souza was quick to get the first word in—loudly. "Tom says Jennifer isn't on the schedule anytime this month. But she could be visiting over at the monastery."

I indicated her abandoned vehicle with a jerk of the head and replied, just as loudly, "Then why'd she leave her car *here*? I'm sure I saw her go inside the Hale."

The man behind the wheel of that other vehicle, an amiable guy of about forty, commented, with a grin, "Dr. Harrel is a walker. If I see her, I'll tell her you're here. Uh . . . our observation period is just beginning. Let's please observe dark skies. No lights, please."

Souza grinned and tossed him a salute. "Right. Thanks a million, Tom. Good viewing. What?—are you on the Schmidt tonight?"

"Yes. We're photomapping for the Hubble space program. God, I hope those crazy hunters don't come back. I've already lost six hours this week to weather and equipment glitches." He pulled slowly away, running without lights.

I went around and slid onto the seat beside Souza. He was grinning like a Cheshire cat. "Lucky strike, eh? He *is* working the Schmidt. They came up to check out the gunfire. I told 'em—"

"What is the Schmidt?" I asked, without really caring.

"I just picked that up," Souza replied smugly. "I guess it's one of the other telescopes; 48-incher, I think. The 'monastery' is where these guys stay while they're on the mountain. Or they call it that. I told 'em—"

I said, "She ran out the other side and into the night, Greg. How big is this place?"

"Big enough," he replied, "that you're not going to find her if she doesn't want you to. What the hell is going on? What're you guys doing up here tonight?"

I replied, "Looking for Donaldson, I guess."

He said, "Shit, that's a waste of time. He hasn't been seen up here for months."

I asked, "So why are you here? And what is this hot talk we need to have?"

"Just scouting," he replied with a sigh. "I get a feeling the roof is falling in and I'd sure like to know where I'm standing so I don't get buried in it." He sighed again, produced a cigarette, lit it. "Something very strange happened up here a few months ago."

I steeled myself for a Souza discourse and lent myself to the game. "What kind of strange?"

"Don't know for sure, just know . . . strange. Donaldson was in on it. He called the President's science advisor, in Washington." A quick flash of the eyes, and: "Yeah, *that* president. Quite a commotion got kicked up. I know the National Security Agency got involved, also the Pentagon and the CIA." Another flash of eyes. "Donaldson also made a few calls outside the country, and it seems that he spent the next several days flying around the country for very hush-hush conferences with other scientists."

I said, "Very interesting."

"Yeah. But wait. It gets more and more. Donaldson dropped out of sight, about that time. So did a guy from M.I.T. and another from Yale. Both theoretical physicists. An exobiologist from somewhere back there also has come up missing. What exactly is an exobiologist? You know?"

I replied, vaguely, "Something about extraterrestrial life, I guess."

"That's what I thought," Souza agreed. "Okay. We also got a guy missing from somewhere out here on the desert, one of those radio astronomers from, uh . . ."

"Socorro?"

"New Mexico, right. You know about that?"

"Not much," I admitted. "It's called a VLA, for 'Very Large Array.' It's a complex of, I don't know, a couple-dozen large dishes linked together over a large area. They're doing some kind of deep-space work out there."

"Military application?"

I shrugged. "What isn't, these days. Maybe so. Star Wars ain't that far off, pal."

"Don't I know it," Souza said glumly. "Well, listen..." He fixed me with a stern gaze. "Since you and the beautiful doc have become so chummy . . . what did she tell you about that incident up here?"

I smiled to myself as I replied to that. "The only 'incident up here' that she mentioned had nothing to do with the present problem, believe it."

"So why'd you come?"

I replied, "She came. I followed, discreetly." I told him about the incident at Glendale and the subsequent events at Malibu, finishing that accounting with: "Looks like whoever it is had a watch on this place, too. You said you were here for a couple of hours. Didn't you notice anything out of focus?—no sense of . . . ?"

Souza replied, "I think those guys followed her from the office area. That's the first I noticed them. She was definitely running. But why run from *me*? Why didn't she run *to* me, for help?"

I said, "Maybe she was just trying to get clear of everyone. I believe she expected to find Donaldson out here. She didn't want to lead anyone else to him."

He commented, "Well, maybe. But I'd sure like to know what happened up here to get the whole damned security apparatus of the nation excited."

"Maybe the flying saucers are coming back," I said, only half-joking.

Souza said, "Aw shit, Ash..."

"Why not?" I asked, not really expecting an answer.

He said, "Are you serious?"

"Would that really surprise you? You want to know something, Greg? I have had my head buried in phenomena my entire adult life. On the scale of things experienced—for me, personally—I would say that a three-dimensional, hard-surfaced alien vehicle in our skies would fall into the class of a very minor phenomenon."

"You're serious as hell, aren't you," he decided.

I was, I hated to admit even to myself, serious as hell. I had done some UFO research in the past—pretty extensively, in a couple of well documented cases; I had even traveled to Europe and South America in the quest for truth in the matter—and my jury was still out.

So I was not ready to buy anything regarding the mystery of Isaac Donaldson. If the man had experienced something strange enough at Palomar to inspire a telephone call to the White House, and then telephone conferences with other scientists around the world—and if a bunch of those learned people were now "missing" with Donaldson...

Well, no, I was not buying anything, yet. But I was not closing the door on anything, either.

CHAPTER NINE
Beneath the Eye

Please don't leap away from me, at this point, if you feel that I am heading into an area of interest which may offend your intellectual or emotional sensibilities. I am trying to present the thing as it presented itself to me—so just bear with me awhile, please, place yourself in my shoes, and enjoy the adventure as I did, without prejudice. Enjoy it, I did, most of it, thoroughly, and I believe that you will, too, if you just give it half a chance.

Anyway, you should not be too stuffy about your own conditioned reality unless lately you have examined it close-up, from the inside out. A common failing among we humans is a penchant for comfort at the expense of something more important than comfort; like, it's easier to sit down and turn the TV on and observe fantasy while dinner turns to fat cells inside our bodies than to run a few laps around the block. We do the same things with our heads, almost as a matter of habit, because we tend to find comfort in the reality that is conditioned by our daily routines.

I'm not saying that's bad: it's probably good, and that is why we do it that way; who wants to go around with his head buried in metaphysical puzzles all the time? I sure don't, but I do try to keep some faint touch with the idea that the sum total of my daily experiences is not nearly large enough to approach anything resembling reality; I therefore live in a conditioned reality which is primarily built of my day-to-day routine.

It's like man's early concepts of cosmology and cosmogony. Cosmology has to do with the theory or philosophy of the nature and principles of the universe. Cosmogony is involved with creation theory, and every religion has one. There was a time, long ago, when the thing that we now call "science" and the thing we call "religion" were one and the same thing. The major schisms now, between science and religion, involve these matters of cosmology and cosmogony—though mainly, I think, cosmogony. But ever since men have been men, probably, there has been this curiosity—innate, no doubt—about how the universe came into being and how it operates.

Early scientists (and I use the term in the broadest sense) were also religionists. Their perceptions of reality, then, usually became codified into a mass of unquestionable dogma which could not be modified without doing damage to the religious edifice—and, since most religions anchor their influence into a good bedrock of divine infallibility, it has been very difficult throughout most of the history of mankind to "change the model" of cosmic reality.

It was the church, remember, that forced Galileo to recant his cosmological theories (though we use those theories to this day in our explorations of space) and it was the church that burned Giordano Bruno at the stake for refusing to recant.

See, there was an intellectual "comfort" in having the earth the center of the universe, a very special creation, instead of being merely one of countless billions of bodies hurtling through space headed God knows where.

You don't have to return to Galileo and Bruno, though,

to find a very deep schism. At this very moment, certain fundamental religionists are greatly concerned over the teaching of evolution in the classroom; they do not agree with the present cosmogonical/cosmological models favored by the same scientific tradition that placed men on the moon. Some of these people, indeed, would burn Darwin at the stake if they could get their hands on him—but see, it's really a question of comfort within a conditioned reality.

Quite a few generations of scientists since Darwin have devoted lifetimes to a meticulous study of that area of reality and consequently could find no comfort whatever in the reality-model of "special creation" (the biblical version). Quite a few generations of religionists since Darwin have kept right on reading their bible and find no comfort whatever in evolution theory.

For myself, I find no controversy there. Science has not yet replaced the Book of Genesis. It has just filled in the blanks—and pardon my ignorance, if that's the problem, but I can see no real conflict between the two accounts.

So I think what it boils down to, probably, is a few diehards who simply find no comfort whatever in the thought that they may be descended from monkeys.

I sort of like monkeys, myself, so . . .

Actually, the evolution model does not say we came from monkeys. Monkeys, and all the other simians, if the model is true, descended with man from a common ancestor—which probably means something worse than monkeys, so what the hell . . .

The only point I'm trying to make is that a conditioned reality can be quite comfortable. We move from one to another with the greatest reluctance, usually. The sad part of that is the fact that most of us get our conditioning by default—that is, from mommy and daddy and aunt julia and father john and nbc/cbs/abc and the national enquirer etc.—instead of sallying forth with an adventurous spirit and an open mind to see what's really out there.

So please do not turn from me in disgust unless you really know where your own reality is coming from.

I would have given a bundle, believe me, to have known where mine was coming from, there in the shadow of the Eye. I am really a very ordinary guy, remember—but saddled with a "gift" that I never asked for in the first place, and one that does nothing but get me in trouble in every other place. So try to have a little sympathy, please, as you watch me struggling through this thing—and save your criticisms for the end.

I did not know what the hell was coming down this pike. It started as a simple "missing person" case. I get a dozen or more of those a year—very routine, even though sometimes very sad as well—but routine in the sense that a common-logic flow of cause/effect events may be tied together with the slightest psychic insight, consisting maybe of no more than a "hunch"—but you can build a great psychic reputation that way. This case began where it should have ended, with the discovery of a corpse. It exploded from there to geeks and spooks, a professional hitman waiting patiently for my head at my driveway, the President of the United States and the entire world intelligence community, a whole gaggle of missing eminent scientists, a creation-physicist with thunder in the valley and a frightened child between the ears, a gun battle beneath the eye of God—and all this coupled to the certain knowledge that this particular reality was expanding at the speed of light because there was no gravitational mass to restrain it.

So don't sneer at me, damn it, for talking about flying saucers. A flying saucer is only marginally more phenomenal than a phantom jet, anyway; it is a difference, primarily, of performance capability, a matter of order of magnitudes somewhat in the same class as the difference between Orville

Wright's Kitty Hawk experience and NASA's Space Shuttle. To a Neanderthal, peering fearfully from his cave at a silver disk hovering directly overhead: okay, yes, phenomenal as hell—but don't smirk at me about flying saucers when I am standing beside a telescope that sees the edge of the universe. The Neanderthal and I do not, thank God, inhabit the same conditioned reality.

If you want to talk "miraculous," then let's please move into the miraculous class. Let's talk about quasars and pulsars, red giants and black holes; let's talk temperatures of 100 million million million million million degrees which, I am told, accompanied the birth of this universe, and let's talk "energy" and "matter" as interchangeable terms for the same stuff depending on temperature. Closer to home, much closer, let's talk about individual atoms created in stars yet used by an exploding ovum to fashion a living being like you or me.

Then let's get down, really down, and talk about a pastoral God who wallowed in the dust of planet earth to bring forth Adam—the same dust, presumably, that He built in the stars—and let us wonder, for just a moment, where the ancients got these fantastic ideas. How did an ancient, prehistoric man ever draw the connection between living flesh and planetary dust? Who told him that? Who told him that there was nothing before a moment of creation, when all around him was abundant evidence of foreverness—and who told him that "the spirit" moved across the flowing rivers of celestial hydrogen (two atoms of hydrogen and one of oxygen, remember, makes water) and separated them to bring forth the world, when clearly, to him, water was water and air was air (firmament) and never the two did occupy the same space at the same time.

You want to talk "miraculous?" Let's talk, then, about an aboriginal tribe in Africa whose oral history traces their origins to a binary-star system in the Pleiades—and their "logo," apparently a star map depicting a binary-star and created many hundreds of years before our own astronomers with their powerful telescopes were able to determine the existence of such a system in Pleiades. Who told them that?

We were discussing conditioned realities, remember. If it is that difficult, and apparently it is, for many modern humans to think freely, imagine how much more difficult it must have been for early men to make the break from the sensible world and to leap the mind into an entirely new and nonsensible world which, nevertheless, was more real than the other.

I am not saying that the "Lord" of Moses was a flying saucer—but it sure sounds like one, and *something* fed those folks in that desert for a couple of generations, "manna" or whatever. I am not saying that the ancient Hindus ever actually got off the ground but the Vedic texts give very convincing descriptions of ". . . an apparatus that moves by inner strength like a bird, whether on earth, in the water or in the air [and] is called a Vimana by the priests of the sciences . . . [and] can move in the sky from place to place, country to country, world to world. . . ." One of the epics purports to give an eyewitness account of a trip in one of these incredible machines, during which the whole earth shrinks beneath its ascent to the size of a ball suspended in space. Again, if it did not happen, who told that ancient poet that the earth would look like that from such a height? If this author was the first science-fiction writer, he is to be congratulated on a superb leap of mind which carried him from virtually the Stone Age to twenty-first-century earth and Star Wars complete with laser weapons and arsenals our own technical genius is still trying to devise.

So. I am standing there beneath the Eye, trying to leap the mind into an understanding of what could have been experienced here that sent a senior scientist scrambling to the White House hotline.

Don't go stuffy on me, please.

My mind has just now begun the leap.

CHAPTER TEN
Vectored

Souza left his car at the Hale and rode with me to the "monastery" for a quick look around. He had been there earlier, a couple of hours before the nightwatch began, and bluffed his way inside—but it probably did not require much bluff because things seemed rather loose in there. The residence probably got its name from a time when just about all astronomers were male—and it was a rather remote site, too far from Cal Tech for daily commuting, so they rotated staff up there and tried to make things as comfortable as possible during the stays on the mountain.

Actually, the place had a sort of traditional "men's club" look—heavy leather chairs, walls of books, that sort of thing. The sleeping quarters were not much, remarkable only for their simplicity and the heavy black shades for daytime sleeping.

Two young men were present—very young men, collegiate—eyeing the bulletin boards when we walked in. Souza and I just acted as though we belonged there, and so did they.

"What's the latest on Halley?" Souza inquired breezily as we walked past.

"Still a fuzzball," one replied, glancing up with an absent grin.

"Big letdown," said the other. "Much ado about popcorn in the sky."

So . . . these kids were not poets. Probably had a bleak future in astronomy, then. Souza and I went on through to the kitchen and got some coffee, carried it with us and sipped at it while we nosed around.

I tried just once, while I was in there, to pick up another fix on Jennifer Harrel but had to withdraw quickly because of the same "static" I'd encountered at the foot of the mountain.

Souza saw me grab my head. "What's wrong?" he growled.

"Some kind of crazy energy enveloping this mountain," I replied, almost groggy from the effect of it. I sat in one of the armchairs and balanced the coffee in my lap for a moment, trying to pull it all back together.

A man of about fifty came into the clubroom while I was seated there, walked over with hand extended to introduce himself. He wore blue jeans, the uniform for this mountain, and a shirt similar to the one Jennifer had worn at our first meeting. He was just "Fred," apparently functioned as some sort of stationkeeper, permanent resident staff.

I shook hands with him and said, "I'm Ford . . . this is Souza. We're meeting Jennifer Harrel."

He raised both eyebrows in an exaggerated show of understanding, replied, "Does she know that?"

I tried to make a rueful smile as I said, "She'd better, after dragging us all the way out here."

He chuckled. "Happens to all of them, once they've been on the mountain. They talk about absentminded professors but star people beat them all." The grin broadened as he dropped the punch line on me. "I just ran her over to Summerfield's for the night."

I said, "She didn't mention . . . ?"

"Nawww, she forgot you. Don't take it personal. You fellas aren't astronomers, are you."

A statement, not a question.

I admitted it. "Just friends. We were going to meet here and get a tour, then on to Summerfield's. Hell, now ... I don't even know how to get to Summerfield's."

"That's easy," Fred assured me. He whipped out a little spiral notebook, made a sketch, tore out the page and handed it to me. "Can't miss it. Big white place, hangs out over the side of the mountain, glass dome on top. Just follow my map. Seven, eight minutes from here."

I persuaded Souza to let me go it alone, much against his better judgment, on the condition that I keep him posted on developments.

"Your mobile phone still on the fritz?" he inquired, eyeing it as we made our way back to the Hale.

I replied, "Yeah, damn thing ... who wants to be tied to a telephone, anyway? Been in the shop twice since—"

"You should get it fixed," he insisted. "Could save your life, one of these days. What's this energy thing you mentioned?"

I told him, truthfully, "Don't know, for sure. Some sort of disturbance, right on my wavelength. This is Indian country, so ... "

He said, "Yeah," as though that explained everything to his satisfaction. As he was transferring to his vehicle, he leaned back to remind me, "Call." He had checked into a motel at Rancho California, on his way up. I had a matchbook in my pocket, with the telephone number printed on it. I promised again to keep him posted. "And watch your ass. Those jerks could still be skulking around here, somewhere."

I doubted that, in view of the wounds. But I promised, also, to watch my ass, then I pulled away and left him standing there in inky darkness beside the eye.

Fred's map was easy to follow; not many roadways across

that mountaintop. I found the place just where he promised I would, and it looked just about the way he'd described it—except that the "glass dome on top" roofed only that portion of the big house that was cantilevered out from the side of the mountain—and the walls of that section were glass, as well. I took a bearing with the compass mounted on the Maserati's dash and decided that these folks could probably see fifty miles into the Pacific from that room on a clear day. A winding drive took me over to it, past several small out-buildings and a twenty-five-foot dish antenna poised to track the heavens; the thing looked to me just a bit too large and considerably more elaborate to be a TV-satellite dish—what the hell, I decided, maybe it's a radio telescope, and why not?

I counted six vehicles parked off to the side—a couple of pickups plus a variety of vans and Jeep types. And the house was even larger than it had appeared from the roadway. Not a lot of light showing from inside, but the tinted-glass of the bubble projection was casting a muted, bluish glow and I could hear faint musical strains from the porch.

A very elderly Indian woman wearing a white uniform-dress responded to my ring and beckoned me to enter without question. It was, by now, an hour past midnight—and there seemed to be a party in progress. I could not see the glass-enclosed room from the entry foyer but I knew where it ought to be and I could hear the murmur of voices from that quarter blending with the soft strains of a Strauss waltz.

If this, I was thinking, was another example of Spartan living supposedly exemplified in the scientific community, then things were definitely looking up for scientists. It was quite a place, easily on a par with the House of Isaac. But, of course, only the twenty-five-foot dish standing outside made any sort of statement relating this residence to the halls of science—so I was just rambling in the mind, and I knew it.

I told the old woman, "I am Ashton Ford. To see Dr. Harrel, please."

Ancient jaws ground an invisible cud as the only direct response to that announcement; she shuffled off without really looking at me, leaving me to wonder if she had heard, or understood, or cared. But another person came down a moment later—neither ancient nor chewing a cud, a dazzlingly beautiful woman of maybe twenty-five with swinging hips encased in denim (what else, on that mountain?), a tank-top thingamajig of some sort of elastic material sculpting magnificent breastworks and a glistening peekaboo belly, bare feet, eyes sparkling with excitement—raven hair, straight and shiny and falling to the hips. She was obviously Indian, or some-such, but she placed a glass of wine in my hand and told me, "I am Laura Summerfield. I sent word to Jen. Won't you come in?"

A voice behind her decided, "No he will not!" in no uncertain tone. It was Jen, herself, of course—very upset and moving quickly to throw the rascal out. She took the wine away from me and returned it to the beautiful Indian maiden, speaking volumes to her in a single look.

Laura made a *faux-pas* face and gracefully withdrew, leaving me to handle Jen's towering wrath on my own.

"What the hell are you doing here!" she hissed, trying to keep the voice down and failing to do so. "Did Souza?—no!—impossible!—that's only been . . . !" She peered at her watch, then scorched me again with those eyes. "Did you follow me? How . . . *disgusting*! How could you do . . . ? Just who the hell do you think you are, Ford?"

"I think," I replied quietly, "I'm the guy who shot a couple of geeks off your back awhile ago. But, of course, if you'd like to rewind and start that frame again . . . "

She said, "Oh," in a small voice, turned away from me, dropped the chin. "I thought Souza did that." She turned back to me, gnawing the lip, said, "It's still a detestable trick. You set me up. Then sat back and watched to see what I would do. I feel like I've been raped."

"I know the feeling," I told her. "Because I did not set you up. I went to my place on the beach, found a dead man waiting for me, beat it back to you as quick as I could, discovered the hard way you'd taken a powder on me, without even a by-your-leave, not a whisper of thanks—just kiss off, buddy boy, and it really was not nice, not very nice at all. So, yeah, maybe I understand the rape feeling."

I did not really feel that way about it, but I wanted her to think I did.

She could not look me in the eye. And the voice, when it came, was contrite without surrender, baffled without surprise. "How did you know I was coming here, then?"

"You don't believe in that stuff," I reminded her, "so just call it a hunch. I'm just glad I wasn't too far behind. Someone has your number, Doc. Any idea who?"

"No, I have no idea who," she replied miserably, suddenly becoming aware of a lot of tension in the neck and trying to placate it with both hands.

I spun her around and went to work on that lovely neck with my own experienced hands. "Look," I told her, "I think I understand what you're going through—to some degree, anyway. I was just kidding about the rape. I don't feel that way. And you're entitled to all the anger you want to put into this thing. But that won't solve anything. You need a friend with a bit of experience in this sort of thing. I like you and I've got the experience. I can be nice, very nice in bed and I'm really great with nervous-tension necks, so . . ."

"You sure are," she said, luxuriating under the massage.

"So what do you say? Want to throw in with me, kid? Say no and I'll walk out the door and never look back. Say yes and I'm in it to the bitter or better end, whichever comes first."

A hint of smile was on the lips as she inquired, "Did you say *better* or *bed her*?"

"That's right," I replied, "whichever comes first."

She laughed, then, that softly melodious sound I was beginning to love and said, "That sounds nice, very nice."

I thought so, too.

Which shows, really, what a lousy psychic I really am.

CHAPTER ELEVEN
The Gathering

I counted fifteen people in the big bubble room, including Jennifer, Laura Summerfield—our hostess—and myself, all male, except for two other attractive women, and all young—midtwenties, say—except for Holden Summerfield, Laura's husband, a distinguished looking gentleman whose age I would peg at about seventy-five. He could easily have been Laura's grandfather—but he was a gracious host and seemed to be interacting comfortably with the others. A California white wine was the prevailing libation and trays of snack foods were scattered about.

It was very definitely a party.

Yet it seemed, somehow, to be something more than that. I could not exactly place a finger on the difference, but it was palpably there nevertheless—something in the very atmosphere of the place, an excitement or a sense of delicious anticipation they all seemed to share. These people were all downright scintillating yet working hard to restrain it—a subdued excitement shining through all attempts to clamp it down.

Jennifer steered me around the room and casually introduced me, first names only, no tags, while Laura moved along in our wake from clump to clump in an apparent follow-up, because I glanced along the backtrack a couple of times to find myself the center of discussion.

The host pumped my hand for about twenty seconds—even he was infected with an almost uncontainable exuberance—while welcoming me to "the gathering" and waggling eyebrows at Jennifer in obvious approval of my presence there. He made me feel like a guest of honor, or something; maybe because I was the only one there, besides himself, not clad in denim.

I don't mind telling you that I was beginning to run out of steam. Starting off with a seven o'clock reveille and progressing through a couple of corpses, a romantic interlude with a creation physicist, two hostile engagements, a brush with the Eye of the Universe, surely several hundred miles behind the wheel of a car, a weird encounter with some form of "psychic static" and an overexposure to Greg Souza's Wacky World of Wonders—it had, all in all, been a hell of a day already and I was starting to fade. I give this, anyway, as an alibi for not tumbling to these people right up front.

About the only parallel that presented itself to me, through that weariness, was a group I once encountered on a hilltop in Brazil. It was the site of some recent UFO encounters, and these folk were gathered there in the joint expectation of another encounter. Those were mostly "peasants," back-country nonsophisticates sprawled upon the hill like so many midnight picnickers, but they had the same look as these obvious sophisticates at this cocktail "gathering" atop Palomar Mountain—a sort of reverent tingling, evidenced mostly in the eyes but also by some strange physical tension that masqueraded as relaxation yet was anything but that. Or maybe I was just hung up on the flying saucer idea. I had always wanted to see one of the damned things, had interviewed hundreds of people who claimed to have seen them, even a couple who claimed to have been aboard one. Maybe I was secretly hoping that I was finally going to see one—or maybe I was simply too damned weary to see what was right there in front of me. At any rate, aside from a fleeting comparison with a UFO-watch, my chief impression of this very attractive group was that they shared some beautiful secret and were just bubbling over with the need to talk about it but didn't quite know how to do so.

Like, maybe, at a college sorority house in which each of the residents had lost her virginity the night before, in a most pleasing way, and was dying to talk about it but afraid to do so. I have never been through that, of course, but I can imagine it and so could you, if you tried. So think of my "gathering" atop Palomar Mountain as a sorority where each of the coeds just had a fling with her own version of Burt Reynolds or Sly Stallone and you will get some idea of the mental atmosphere.

But I was too tired to dope it. I stood at the glass wall with Jennifer and asked, quietly, "Can we see Hawaii on a clear day?"

She laughed softly. "I guess you can see whatever you'd like to see."

"Don't I wish," I muttered.

"You're intimidated again," she scolded playfully.

"Who are these people?"

"Friends."

"Scientific-type friends?"

"Mostly, yes."

I was thinking that the median age for scientists must be shrinking like crazy. And no wonder. They'd been cradle-robbing "exceptional" students for years, now, slapping them into university programs almost before they were old enough to stay out alone after dark. The only person in that whole crowd with any seasoned maturity was Laura's husband— and I didn't have his pedigree, yet.

And, yes, that turned out negative. "Summerfield?" I inquired, continuing the dialogue.

"One, yes; the other, no. Laura is a microbiologist. Holden is just Holden, quite wealthy—but he does have an avocational interest in astronomy."

"Is that a radio telescope I saw out there?"

"Yes. Quite sensitive."

I tried a shot. "But, of course, nowhere in the same league as the VLA at Socorro."

She stared at me for a moment, then: "You are a constant amazement to me, Ashton. No, not in the same league. But it does have an excellent cryogenics unit and he has been doing some very interesting private research."

I asked, "Into what?"

"Microwave radiation background," she replied tersely.

"Meaning," I pursued, "the big-bang residual."

"I do believe," she said, rather tartly, "you are trying to impress me, Ashton. Really, it is not necessary. Please do not be intimidated by—"

"I believe," I interrupted, "that you are patronizing me. Really, I feel no need to impress you or anyone. I am trying to get a feel of my environment. Who are these people? What are they secretly gloating about? What is a twenty-five-foot dish with a cryogenics unit doing here in this man's backyard and why is he privately researching an area that has been thoroughly covered by the best minds in science? Where the hell is Isaac and what does this midnight gathering here at the edge of the earth have to do with his disappearance?"

Her eyes were wide and glistening as I concluded my little speech. "Oh, my," she commented humorously, "we do take our job seriously. Really, Ashton . . ."

I was getting steamed, and I still don't know why. "Don't do that, Jen," I growled. "There's no 'job' involved here and you know it. Get it through your head, damn it, that we are in a highly dangerous situation. You have been attacked directly twice this day and there is evidence that spooks of every stripe are swarming all over us. So—"

"What exactly do you mean by *spooks*?"

"Spies, agents, operatives—by whatever name, *spooks*. Souza has found reason to wonder if his own mysterious retainer is Russian and—"

"But that's ridiculous! Isn't it?"

"Maybe not. I told you I'd found a corpse at my place in Malibu. Before that became a corpse it was lately believed to be a professional murderer and maybe taking orders from the CIA. The thing is, he was waiting there for me with a silenced pistol when someone else took him out of the game. If this guy *was* CIA, and if Souza's entry into the case *was* via the KGB or whoever, then that particular incident makes some kind of crazy sense—and I can't make any other sense out of it. So this game, whatever it is, is being played in blood and you can bet that great ass of yours that none of these guys gives a particular damn about whose blood it is. So don't talk *job* to me. All the money in the world couldn't interest me in a game like this one. What is holding me here, Jen, is *not* a *job*."

"What is, then? My great ass?"

I smiled faintly and said, "Sorry."

"You're just upset again."

"Something like that, yeah. Point is, kiddo, you're playing tea-party with me while the sky is falling. If I'm *in*, then I have to be *clear* in. So let's get me cleared, damn it, with whoever's in charge of this game."

She was wavering and I could see it.

But then the beauteous Laura came over to join us, towing another junior scientist—a rather commanding looking guy to whom I had not yet been introduced.

"Ashton, you haven't met Esau yet, have you. Esau, Ashton."

He gave me a warm, tight grip and a nice smile. I said,

"That's an interesting name. Don't believe I've ever encountered it, outside the bible."

"Oh, you read the bible," he murmured.

"Now and then," I admitted.

He said, "Laura tells me you're a noted psychic detective."

Something about the way this guy formed his words or chose his words, or something in the speech, put me off just a bit. It wasn't exactly stilted. Just . . . odd. I told him, "That is either a kindly exaggeration or a nasty libel, depending upon the point of view. What's yours?"

He was all smiles. "I love it. Always wanted to meet a psychic."

"Me, too," Laura bubbled. "I was positively fascinated a few years ago by an article on this man—what's his name, the famous European psychic who works with the police to solve murders and all that. Is that what you do?"

I said, "Not exactly. And I'm not exactly a detective. More like a consultant, really. I don't know how much of what I do is psychism and how much is lucky blundering. I don't read other people's minds, if that's what you're wondering."

"I'll bet you do," she replied with a mischievous twinkle.

I don't know why I suddenly felt so candid, but I told her, "Well at least you're safe, here on this mountain. The whole area seems bathed in some strange energy that cannot be psychically penetrated."

You would have thought I'd cussed Einstein, or something, from the reaction I got to that. The twinkle and the smile and everything animated faded from that pert face, something that almost groaned moved deep within the dark eyes, and she asked me, very soberly, "How does that affect you?"

I replied, just as soberly, "Not at all, unless I open to it. Then it nearly knocks me off my feet. Know what could be doing that?"

She stared at me for a very long moment, consulted Esau with eyes only, then turned to Jen and quietly advised her,

"Better tell him." She gave me a final sober, sorrowing sweep of the eyes as she walked away.

Esau said, in that strangely ponderous speech, "Yes, Jennifer, I'm afraid you must tell him." He showed me a sympathetic look, placed an untouched glass of wine in my hand, and hurried after Laura.

I said to Jennifer, "Tell him, then."

She was all torn up inside. "I—I really—I need to know more about you, Ashton. This is—oh damn!—can I really trust you?"

I told her, "I believe you have to."

"Give me a cigarette," she commanded irritably.

I did so, and one to myself, lit them both, gently urged, "Tell him, Jen."

She took a deep pull at the cigarette, exhaled the smoke in a burst toward the tinted glass dome, eyed me up and down—said, very quietly, "It's a previously unknown form of radiant energy."

"What is?"

"What do you mean, *what* is. The thing you mentioned, the strange energy. It is a previously unknown form of radiant energy."

I tasted Esau's wine and asked her, "Previous to what?"

She replied, almost angrily, "Previous to its discovery, here, on this mountain, a few months ago."

"How was it discovered?"

She just glared at me.

"Isaac," I guessed, though it was a fairly well-educated guess.

She nodded the troubled head.

I asked her, "Is it something in the earth around here or . . . ?" I lifted my gaze to the dome.

She replied, "No, it's nothing in the earth. The source is extraterrestrial."

I said, "That does not exactly pinpoint anything, does it."

She raised her shoulders and dropped them, turned away from me, took another pull at the cigarette.

I took another pull at the wine and said, "Well, damn it, make up your mind. Am I nice, or not."

Those shoulders began to quiver. She turned back to me with a suppressed giggle, said, "You *do* give great foot."

I said, "Thanks."

"And I guess you really are very nice."

"Thanks again. So tell the nice man, Jen. What the hell is going on, here? And why is it suddenly so important that I be told about it?"

She sobered abruptly, said, "I suppose Laura thinks it could be dangerous for you."

"Laura is exactly right," I said. "And it is getting more dangerous by the second. I am in imminent danger of exploding all over you. What the hell are we talking about?"

"Ashton . . . this is terribly important. And terribly delicate. We have to be very careful . . . well, you've already seen the results of the official reaction . . . We simply cannot let global politics take this over. That is why Isaac went into hiding." She raised both arms in a sweep of the room. "All of these people are in hiding, too. They are friends of Isaac. And they are all working with Isaac in an attempt to understand this . . . what is happening here."

I asked, softly, "What *is* happening here, Jen?"

She replied, "Palomar Mountain is being irradiated from a point in space and . . . "

I said, "A *point* in space?"

"Yes. Not deep space, either. Local space."

"From within the solar system," I suggested.

"Yes. It is being experienced as a beam. Well, as two beams. One appears to be targeted here, on Palomar. The other target is in Russia."

I decided I already knew where, in Russia. "Caucasus Mountains," I ventured.

"At Zelunchukskaya, yes, their version of Palomar."

I said, "The obvious significance of that, then . . ."

She said, "Yes. The beams are obviously intelligently directed."

I asked, "Why? By whom?"

"That is what we are hoping to determine," she replied quietly.

"And how do you go about doing that?" I wondered aloud.

"The answer," she said, "may be in the beams themselves."

But it was not in the cards for me to get any closer to that answer, myself, right away.

The room was beginning to tilt. Something was wrong with my eyes. I looked at Jennifer, then into Esau's wineglass, noted that I had emptied it, began making the connection just as the room began fairly spinning around me.

The gathering of scintillating scientists were now gathering around me, and some were reaching out to me, supporting me, keeping me from spinning off to wherever the rest of the room was going. I groaned, "Damn it, Jen . . ."

"It's okay," she told me in a very soothing manner. And that was the last sound I heard before I spun off into cosmos.

CHAPTER TWELVE
In the Eyes Of...

I dreamed that I'd finally gotten my wish and not only saw a flying saucer but was actually aboard one. It looked suspiciously like Holden Summerfield's glass bubble room, though, and every member of the crew scintillated with the same constrained excitement noted in his guests at the gathering. Holden himself was aboard. I think he was an admiral, or whatever corresponds to admiral in the inter-galactic fleet, because his white uniform was resplendent with radiant stars. He was a forty-eight-star admiral, and that's a lot more rank than anyone down here ever saw. I noticed for the first time, in that dream, how closely Holden resembled C. Aubrey Smith—but that probably would mean nothing to you unless you're an old-movie buff like me.

Esau was the command pilot but he was wearing a really weird uniform made of goat skins—and I kept asking him, "Are you Esau or are you Jacob?" but he kept ignoring the question and dunking ambrosia in wine and trying to get me to share it with him. I was having none of that—we all know that ambrosia makes you immortal and I was not about to go for that until someone told me where we were headed.

I am a bit embarrassed to relate the rest of the dream because it got highly erotic. I will just say, here, that Laura was involved, clad only in her long shiny hair but grown considerably longer so that it was pulled up through her thighs like a loin cloth, on between humongous breasts and tied with a pretty denim bow behind her neck. There was something even stranger about Laura, though—some vague problem having to do with what lay beneath all that hair; suffice it to say that I was having trouble with a connection. There was a deep sorrow in her eyes, probably because of that, and she kept murmuring over and over, "She should have told you."

The dream was so vivid that I had trouble making the transition to the waking state. I was lying on a hospital bed in a brightly sunlit room, Laura was bending over me in a white smock, and I had her hair in both my hands. She laughed softly and asked me, "Are you awake? Do you know where you are?"

I replied, with a mouth full of mush, "Hell, I'm sorry, kid, but I just can't find it."

She laughed again, freed her hair from my grasp, and told me, "Well whatever you're looking for, you won't find it in there. I'll have you know I brush my hair a hundred strokes every morning and every night."

It all came back to me, then. I shoved her away from me, I guess a bit too forcefully, and sat bolt upright on the bed. She sort of hit the wall and gave a little shriek. Two guys came running in from somewhere and gave me a hard but somewhat undecided look.

"It's okay, it's okay," Laura assured them. "He just awoke with a bit of confusion. Let's get some food in here, now. And coffee, right away."

"No ambrosia," I added thickly.

The guys grinned and went back out.

Laura stood at the wall, arms folded across that magnificent chest, and said, "You'll have to forgive my bedside manner. I do have an M.D. but I haven't really practiced it."

"Don't worry about it," I growled. "You'll probably grow up to be a pretty good doctor some day." My head was booming, hangover style. I held it in both hands to keep it from falling off my shoulders and asked her, "What did you people give me? How'd you get this jackhammer in here between my ears?"

She said, "Sorry about the headache. It will pass soon, once we get some food into you. You're going to be just fine."

I said, "I was just fine last night when I walked in here."

"That wasn't last night," she informed me.

I glanced at my bare wrist, cast about for my watch, located it on the bedside table, succeeded in focusing one eye on the tiny day/date display. Damn. It was Monday already.

"What happened to Sunday?" I asked her.

"Sorry, we had to check you out thoroughly. That's what happened to Sunday."

An Indian woman came in with a tray, placed it beside me and withdrew without looking directly at me. I realized only then that I was totally naked. The tray had coffee, two cups, cream and sugar—silver service. I repositioned the sheet about me and swung my legs over the side of the bed. That was a mistake. I hung onto the bed for dear life while Laura poured the coffee. She held the cup to my lips for a couple of sips.

"Bathroom," I croaked.

"Are you nauseous?" she inquired, properly concerned about that, as she helped me to my feet.

"Piss call," I replied.

She laughed softly and steered me into the proper direction, suggested, "A shower could help."

I reached back for the coffee and carried it with me to the

bathroom, gaining stability as I went and not the least embarrassed about my nakedness, hard-on and all.

And, yeah, the shower did help—but not the hard-on, the piss call took care of that, but five minutes beneath a near-scalding spray unkinked the brain and rekindled the circulation. I came out of it beet-red all over and feeling almost human again, pardon the expression. The coffee had cooled so I gulped it down, cinched a towel at the waist and stepped out for a refill. Laura was seated beside the bed, cup poised at pouted lips but nothing happening there, engrossed in some dark mental study.

She looked up as I filled my cup, said, lightly, "Well thank God you've found your modesty."

I clucked my tongue at her and replied, "And you a medical doctor."

"Told you I haven't really practiced," she said soberly. "Truly, Ashton, you're a hell of a turn-on."

I gave no response to that, verbally or otherwise, but returned to the bathroom with my coffee, for a shave. Had to wonder, though, about her obviously mismatched marriage and the possible stresses therefrom; wondered, also, how much of my dream had been pure fantasy and how much . . .

But I chased that away. It wasn't fair, I knew, to speculate about such matters, not even in the privacy of one's own mind. I felt it okay, though, to relate that whole idea to my observations on Jennifer. Both of these young women apparently possessed a surprising sexual energy, or maybe it was merely a sexual forthrightness, a proper recognition of an entirely natural human process. Call it a good attitude about sex.

Or was that really the case? Did it have something to do with this *Bride of Science* idea? Was it a healthy attitude or was it downright horniness born of frustration?

In a way, I decided, Laura Summerfield was in about the same sexual boat as Jennifer Harrel. For a bright young female scientist, maybe marriage to a sweet and supportive grand-fatherly man was tantamount to remaining a Bride of Science. But who the hell was I to hand down that kind of decision? What did I know about it? Different people marry for different reasons—and different people fall in love with different attributes. So what if a beautiful young woman gets turned on occasionally to an exciting young man? That's not love, it's chemistry. It may take some really rare attributes of the male character to turn that same young woman's thoughts to true love—attributes, perhaps, found only in a truly mature man. So what, then, if he happens to be mature enough to be her grandfather. And whoever said that sex is dead in the rocking chair. I'd known some pretty damn feisty old . . .

Jennifer had intimated a very strong affection for Isaac, even to the point of suggesting that she would marry him if he were so inclined. I supposed that Isaac and Holden were roughly the same age; ditto for Jennifer and Laura. In Jennifer's case, I'd assumed hero-worship had something to do with it—but what the hell—reflecting on that, I decided there was not a hell of a lot of difference between hero-worship and being in love. Wasn't that what every guy who ever lived really wanted: to be worshiped like a God by his woman?

Laura was fussing with the bed when I finished with the bathroom. Apparently she'd changed the sheets and was now in the process of installing clean pillow slips. I went to the window to orient myself, assuming that this room was some-where in the Summerfield mansion. It was, off to the side and somewhat below the cantilever. I could see the tinted blue glass of the bubble room; it seemed even more imposing by daylight—and, yeah, not too unlike the popular concep-tion of a flying saucer. I chuckled and turned away from the window, almost colliding with Laura, who apparently had planned on joining me there. We still wound up belly to belly—or belly to towel—and it seemed the only natural thing to place my hands on her shoulders. Her hands found my hips as she inquired, "What's funny?"

"Crazy dream I had," I told her. "Am I a prisoner here?"

She replied, "Of course not. But we would like for you to stay with us for awhile."

"That's nice," I said. "Why?"

"You could become a highly valuable addition to our team."

"You don't even know what position I play."

"I know more about you than you may realize," she replied with a mischievous flare of the eyes.

I asked, "How much do you know about Isaac?"

"Oh, much more than that."

"I've never seen the man. Have I?"

She pursed those ripe lips and replied, "Gosh, I don't know. Have you?"

"Does he look anything like C. Aubrey Smith?"

She laughed. "Who?"

I amended that. "Like Holden."

"Oh no, I wouldn't say so. I know who C. Aubrey Smith is. The very dignified British actor. He was British, wasn't he? You know, come to think of it, Holden does look like him. Not Isaac, though. Isaac looks like, let's see . . ." Those dark eyes were fairly atwinkle, obviously enjoying the game. "Remember the man who played the older doctor on Ben Casey?"

I said, "Dr. Zorba. He was played by Sam Jaffe."

"Right!" she said triumphantly, making it about a four-syllable word. "Such a dear. Now *that* is Isaac."

I thought, well shit, so much for exploding theories. I had been sort of toying with the notion that Isaac Donaldson and Holden Summerfield could be one and the same person, that neither of these young ladies was actually married to either. After all, I knew only what I had been told. They could tell me anything, for the sake of cover.

Of course, they could still be doing that.

I asked her, "Who played the title role in the 1930s Hollywood production of *Gunga Din*?"

She said, "Are we playing trivia now?"

"It's a test," I told her.

"Okay, I give up. I can see him very clearly in my mind, but . . ."

I said, "Same guy. Sam Jaffe. Many years before Dr. Zorba."

She said, "I'll be darned!"

I said, "Yeah. I'm a little surprised that you know about Zorba *or* Gunga Din. I mean, even Zorba is going back quite a few years."

"Not on my television," she declared brightly. "I can see him any morning at three o'clock. And I watched *Gunga Din* on videocassette at my last encampment, just last year. But, gosh—well, you know, I *do* remember looking at old Gunga and thinking there was something familiar in the eyes, something . . ."

Yes, that's what was bothering me. Something in the eyes. I was looking into hers as I asked, "Who is Esau?"

She blinked. "I introduced you Saturday night."

I said. "Yeah. Who is he?"

"He's . . . well he's part of our team."

"What's he do?"

"At the moment, for us, he is engaged in spectroscopic studies."

"And what are you engaged in?"

"Living waves."

"What?"

"Well . . . biological energy studies."

"Living waves sounds better," I told her. "Let's stick with that. Find any inside me?"

"You bet I did," she replied soberly.

"Healthy?"

"Terribly."

"What sort of radiation have I been exposed to?"

She hesitated briefly, then: "That kind, yes."

Her hands had slowly inched along beyond my hips and were now pressing rather insistently against my backside. I was terribly, warmly aware of her growing pressure at my front side. My towel fell away. She nuzzled my ear and whispered, "*Jesus*, Ashton."

Before I could respond in any way whatever, she pushed her way clear and hurried out of there without a backward look.

I retrieved the towel, tried to make it tent back around me but it would not.

I would, I decided, take that cold shower now.

I just wished that she'd turned back for one more look. I wanted to see again if I'd seen what I thought I saw in those deep, dark eyes.

Something there, yeah, for sure . . . something in the eyes.

Only then did it register, her final statement before the crazies started: "That kind, yes."

What kind, damn it! We'd been talking about radiation and living waves. *That* kind!

I decided to take that back to the shower with me, too, with "something in the eyes."

"Living wave" radiation, eh? Fancy that.

CHAPTER THIRTEEN
Making Waves

I don't know if I have mentioned, yet, that I am sort of a scientist myself. The largest problem in my life, I guess, is that I am "sort of" many things. Guess I just have too many interests. Never could seem to focus myself into any one career-slot long enough to become expert in it. Then, too, I never really felt the financial pressure—that hungry feeling, as some have expressed it—which sometimes will keep one's nose to a grindstone. I am fortunate—or unfortunate, however it strikes you—to have come into a tidy little trust, funded in my behalf before I was born or even conceived, which takes care of my basic needs 'til death do us part— and I am not really a greedy person, have no particular desire to amass a fortune of my own ... so what the hell, I kicked back a long time ago and decided to just let the world come to me as it would.

The navy time was my only long-term commitment to anything—but I was actually set up for that before my birth, too. It's the Ashton family tradition. Each male son in the line is born with a silver anchor up his ass, and he can take it out only upon graduation from Annapolis. Big deal, you may say, poor kid—has to put in four whole years of an otherwise dissolute life at a tuition-free college—not only tuition-free but they give you a salary, to boot, and a guaranteed career job upon graduation.

Which is fine, sure, if that's where your interests lie. Problem with me was that my interests lay everywhere *but* in a naval career—and there is that matter of the years of obligated service after you graduate. So I simply tried to make the best of it, spread myself out as much as I could, took every class, every war college I could finagle my way into. Along the way, I became a little bit of everything and not a hell of a lot of anything. Which is where I'm at right now.

I have a basic grounding in the physical sciences and a touch here and there in the theoretical extensions. I can converse reasonably intelligently in the language of mathematics. I can even converse reasonably intelligently with digital computers and have a real party with analog computers. It is possible for me, in certain situations, to stand toe to toe with theoretical physicists and to at least give the impression that I know what they are talking about. I give you all this just so you will know where I am coming from in that which follows.

Because, I have to be right up front with you, I still did not know what the hell was coming down that pike at Palomar. Okay, sure, "a previously unknown form of radiation" may sound rather bland—but, hey, we are talking last-quarter twentieth-century, the age of space, the world that Einstein and Planck and Bohr have defined for us. We even have people on this planet who are arguing (and very intelligently) over the exact temperature of the primordial universe at the precise one-one-millionth of a second after the expansion began. They stopped arguing quite awhile ago over the precise contents of the universe, or the nature of nature, after the first one-hundredth of a second.

We are talking "creation physics" now, and these people

are measuring time and events by the hundredths of a second—a time that began perhaps fifteen billion years before they were even born.

So, yes, it can be a rather astounding statement to have one of these brilliant folk casually remark that a "previously unknown" form of radiant energy has just been found out. I am sure it was rather astounding to all of them, as well, in view of the fact that they had already very neatly bundled up all the contents of this universe as of the first minute of creation.

A "previously unknown" factor could wreak considerable havoc upon the structure of everything else they thought they'd known. Unless...

Unless, of course, this was not merely a "previously unknown" force but something totally new in the universe. And something "new," in this 15-to-20-billion-year-old structure—I mean something intrinsically new, some new nature of nature—would, it seemed to me, have the very deepest ramifications for mankind.

So that is where I was at, in trying to make sense of Laura Summerfield's surprising hint that this supposedly intelligently directed irradiating beam was a "living wave." What the hell did that mean?

I need to talk to you for just a moment about wave dynamics. Rather than go into a deeply technical discussion, let me just say—and it is probably safe to do so—that virtually everything that moves, vibrates, or "shines" does so accompanied by a "wave." There are sound waves, light waves, electric waves, magnetic waves, even gravitational waves; in the new quantum physics, all radiant energy is defined in terms of wave*lengths* which are determined by the energy and momentum of elementary particles which— embedded within and apparently responsible for *waves*—behave as sheer energy.

But now, as for this matter of *living waves*—biological

matter is put together using the same elementary particles as those found in ordinary matter. The cells of your body are built of atoms that are manufactured inside of stars, those atoms are composed of elementary particles such as protons and electrons, various quarks and widgets and whatever, and each of these is subject to the same laws that govern the behavior of elementary particles everywhere.

Our very *brains* vibrate with energy waves. The brain *wave* is that which is being measured by an electro-encephalograph. So-called *beta* and *alpha* rhythms are simply characteristic states of what may be called wave systems produced within the brain. There has been nothing to indicate—in my understanding, anyway—that brain waves are significantly different from other energy waves, however. The EEG actually measures changes in electric potential, which is essentially the story of radiant energy anywhere.

So what is a *living* wave?

The late Carnegie scientist Gustaf Stromberg, as long ago as the early 1940s, hypothesized an "immaterial living structure" which is responsible for the intelligent organization of living matter at the cellular level, and spoke of "the autonomous field" as something which "must be of a very profound nature, since it must in some way or other be associated with the ultimate origin of energy, matter, life, and mind." His autonomous field produces immaterial structures which may be thought of as living waves—and Stromberg spoke also of ". . . a world intimately connected with our own consciousness." I have found no evidence that this particular aspect of his work has seized the imagination of other scientists or even their respect; I do know that flags flew at half-mast in his native Sweden when he died.

So much for that. I had worse problems at hand. Jennifer Harrel, for instance. Obviously she had not been entirely honest with me. No—that is too kind—she had lied like hell to me, deliberately, with purpose. I wished to believe that her motives were all good, in that respect. Her chief concern, rightfully so, was the security of Isaac Donaldson and this program of his, whatever it was. She knew that I had been retained to ferret him out. Right away that made us antagonists. It is perfectly understandable, then, that she did everything in her power to lead me *away* from Isaac rather than toward him. I could understand and accept all that. What I could *not* accept was the very shaky foundation upon which I had been building my understanding of this case; everything I knew or thought I knew could be false.

That is not the most comfortable place to be—perched up there on a mountaintop surrounded by scintillating strangers, all of whom could be playing some weird game which I perhaps would not understand even if I knew all the rules and conditions.

I had the very strongest urge to get the hell away from there—to call everyone I had ever known or had even been introduced to in Washington—to blow the whistle on this whole operation—to let the pieces fall where they may.

But, damn it... Something in the eyes, maybe. Some deep sadness, or... What the hell was it about these people that put them so much beneath my skin?

Esau, now... that guy really bugged me. But not in any way I could grab with the mind. He seemed a nice young man, engaging, quick, attractive—but something in the *manner*, and maybe that was it, all of it—despite the blue jeans and Pendleton shirt, the guy seemed to have just emerged from an Edwardian parlor or some such damn...

And Laura, now *there* was something very different, an absolutely flaming beauty, fairly oozing sexuality, but those same eyes, a look of... of what? Wise, yeah. She looked *wise*. And that, somehow—to my sense of harmony, anyway—I'm talking *old* wise, wisdom—but a sort of *sad* wisdom—that, to me, was out of place with the rest of the package.

I could not leave it at that. I could not leave, period. I was not so sure they would allow me to leave, despite Laura's recent assurance that I was not a "prisoner."

So I was stuck with these people, for better or for worse—or, at least, until more "worse" showed up.

For the moment, anyway, I would give them the benefit of the doubt.

I just hoped they wouldn't end up whisking me away to another world, in another galaxy, at the far edge of the universe. Or, God forbid, to a totally different universe.

CHAPTER FOURTEEN
Holy Grams

A wheeled serving cart laden with fruit, ham and eggs, juices
and fresh coffee was waiting for me when I quit the bathroom
that second time. I attacked it voraciously and very quickly
dispatched everything there except for an apple and a banana
which I stashed for later. I felt better after the first bite and
was fairly bursting with energy when I got up from there.

My clothing, freshly cleaned, was laid out for me on the
bed. I put everything on and went adventuring. Could not
find anyone to adventure with, though, until I got to the
bubble room. Holden was there, staring rather absently at an
issue of *Sky & Telescope* magazine. He dropped the magazine
at my approach and sprang to his feet with surprising agility
to greet me, very solicitous, those great eyebrows dancing
with every word and gesture.

I assured him that I was okay and that I was being marvelously taken care of, thanked him for his hospitality, asked
if I might use the phone. He gave grand permission and led
me to it. I climbed onto a bar stool and punched the number
for the motel in Rancho California while Holden discreetly
returned to his chair near the window.

Souza had checked out of that motel on Sunday.

So I tried his office, spoke briefly to Foster, was passed on through to a very grouchy private detective.

"Where the hell are you?" he snarled.

I said, "Still on the mountain. I see you've gone home."

"Why not? No percentage in me hanging around . . ."

I reminded him, "Thought home was a bit too hot for you."

He growled, "So I cooled it and came home. What're you up to?"

I told him, "I've been unconscious since about one o'clock Sunday morning."

"You sure have," he sniffed.

"Literally," I told him. "Can't explain it any better than that right now but . . . how did you cool it?"

"Finally got to the right people," he replied, still sulking. "Don't worry, I cooled it for you, too."

I said, "Thanks. Well I—"

"Don't tell me anything, Ash. I don't want to know anything. I'm off the case."

I asked him, "That's how you cooled it?"

"In a manner of speaking, yeah. I suggest you come home, too."

"Can't do that," I told him.

"Your retainer expired at seven o'clock this morning. So you're on your own."

I said, "Okay. No big loss, Greg. You don't pay too well, pal, when you pay at all."

He protested, "I don't owe you a damn . . ."

"Maybe you do," I told him. "You brought me into this mess. If I have to fight my way out of it . . ."

"You don't have to do that."

"For my own peace of mind, yes I do. I want some information from you."

"Don't have a hell of a lot." But he was lightening up.

"You mentioned the other night that some other scientists were missing."

"Yeah."

"Who are they?"

"Hell I don't have their names."

"Do you remember how many?"

A pause, then: "Dozen or so, I guess. From . . . "

I reminded him, "Yeah, you said from M.I.T. and Yale, I think, some other places. You don't remember any names?"

"I don't know that I even *had* any names," he replied.

"How about Russia?"

"Look, Ash . . . I'm already in violation of my—I can't discuss this matter."

I said, "We're not discussing that matter, then, Greg. We're just talking science stuff. Like, maybe, a group of whiz kids. Is that what we're talking about?"

"*Whiz* kids? I don't believe so, no. I had the impression these were senior people. Like Don—the other guy."

"You sure about that?"

"No. I'm not sure of anything."

I said, "Russia?"

He said, "Uh, I think—you know, Ash, anything happens in this country usually happens over there, too."

I said, "Okay. Thanks. Take care."

"You, too," he replied, and hung up.

I sat there chewing that conversation for a minute or two, then decided I wanted one with Holden, too. Before I could make a move, though, Esau came gliding up behind me and gave a warm squeeze to my shoulder as he settled onto the stool beside me.

"Sorry," he said quietly, "I am afraid no one thought of the possibility that you may have someone to worry about you." He placed a leather folder on the bar and tapped it with a delicate finger. "Nothing in here to indicate it."

I said, dryly, "You have my dossier."

"Nothing quite that formal," he said, smiling. "But we did feel it imperative that we have your medical records, that sort of thing."

I asked him, "How many sorts outside of medical?"

He raised eyebrows at me, started to question the question, then checked himself with a smile and replied, "You are very perceptive. Yes, of course, we did run a thorough background check on you."

"How'd I come out?"

He laughed softly, nodded his head several times—actually, the whole upper part of his body nodded—then replied, "I would say quite well, quite well indeed. Almost a Renaissance man, aren't you?"

I said, "Well, I try."

"You could have had an impressive career in science."

I said, "Never really wanted that. Actually, I think I would like to conduct the Boston Pops. Or maybe the New York Philharmonic."

He stared at me quizzically for a moment, then his eyes strayed to the leather folder. "I found nothing concerning musical ability."

So my humor was lost on this guy. I told him, "All of the ability is in appreciation, I'm afraid. But I do listen one hell of a great French horn and sometimes an entire string section in the bargain."

He had not the foggiest notion of what the hell I was talking about, I could see that in the eyes, but he laughed anyway and said, "Well, hobbies are nice but the work is what it is all about. Have you found that so?"

I said, "Is that with a capital 'W'?"

He laughed some more, said, "So right, so right"—then suddenly became very serious: "We believe that you could be an asset to our research. We would like for you to join us. For a few days, at most."

I said, "Think you can drain the whole brain in just a few days, eh?"

The look he gave me was totally blank as he replied, "We really would like to know how the field interacts with your extrasensory perception. We have already devised the tests. A few days, at most, should satisfy all our questions."

I said, very quietly, "Let me think about it, Esau."

"Certainly, Ashton, certainly. Think about it. I will speak to you again at dinner." He slid off the stool, turned back to retrieve his leather folder, showed me a charmer smile.

I asked him, very quietly, "Ever been aboard a flying saucer?"

He replied, just as quietly, "No, and I should think I would not wish to attempt it."

"Why not?" I asked soberly.

"I am having a bit of trouble with you, Ashton," he said. "I never learned sophisticated repartee, you see. I rather grew up in the very lap of science."

I grinned and said, sincerely, "Sorry, Esau. I was not trying to put you down, please believe that. I imagine you have a real rapier thrust with field equations."

He smiled back. "I am much more at home there, yes, thank you. As for riding a flying saucer, I doubt that you would enjoy it."

Again, I asked, "Why?"

He replied, "Because if such a thing exists, as it has been universally described in the reports, it is no more than a three-dimensional hologram."

I said, "Really."

He said, "Yes. Consider the motions that have been reported. Fluttering, swinging, precise ninety degree turns at great speeds, instant dislocation and reappearance in a different sector, sudden appearance and disappearance. Each such motion is physically impossible in Newtonian physics, as that relates to mass and momentum. However . . ."

"A holographic image, however . . ."

"Yes, very good, you have my meaning already. A reflective surface, such as a mirror or a crystal, will focus light rays over considerable distances, and the merest vibration of the reflector will cause the light image to shimmer or flutter, to race about in senseless patterns this way and that, to fairly dance, to appear and disappear as though in total defiance of Newtonian physics. Of course, there is no actual mass involved, so . . ."

I said, "So someone is playing tricks with giant mirrors in the sky."

"I am suggesting no such thing," he replied primly. "Nature herself plays such *tricks* all the time. Who has never seen a rainbow? Have you noticed that the classic representation of a flying saucer looks very like a spiral galaxy in one of our photographs from earth? Under certain conditions, our atmosphere can become highly prismatic. It takes no great stretch of the imagination to infer a holographic image of a spiral galaxy as the perfect solution to all purported sightings of flying saucers. Night or day, I might add."

I said, "Yes, that's very interesting. But what about encounters of the second and third kind?"

"That falls under a whole different class of phenomena. You'll have to speak to the behavioral scientists about that."

I said, quietly, "Mental phenomena, mass hallucinations, that sort of thing."

"I should think so, yes." He picked up the folder, tucked it beneath his arm. Had he been wearing a hat, he would have tipped it, I'm sure. "Well. See you at dinner, Ashton."

I watched him walk away and kept on staring after him long after he disappeared from view.

And I felt better, somehow. Yes. I was really glad to have had that most illuminating conversation with my old friend Esau. Or was it Jacob, in goatskins?

Naw. Naw. It was Esau.

CHAPTER FIFTEEN
The Crucible

I asked Holden, "All those people I met the other night—are they staying here with you? All of them?"

He waggled his eyebrows at me as he replied, "Why, yes, I believe—let me see—I think so, yes. Don't remember just who all was here, you see, but . . . "

"But you do have a house full of guests?"

"That is my good fortune, yes."

I asked him, "Where are they now?"

The eyebrows kept right on twitching. "Working, I would think." He laughed heartily. "I would *hope*."

"I mean, where? Where are they working?"

"Oh, in the *lab*." He gazed about him as he laughed some more. "Couldn't expect them to just flop about here in the club, could we."

Very jovial fellow. I asked him, "Where is the lab, Holden?"

He sprang to his feet again. "What an *ass* I am!" He was actually embarrassed, beet-red. "Of *course* you haven't seen the lab yet. Dear me. I'm getting old, Ashton. Senile, I do believe." He had me by the arm. "We'll just take care of—"

"No no, that's okay," I protested. "Actually I'd like to just sit down and talk with you for awhile. The lab, later."

He released me, with a delighted grin, and sat himself down abruptly like an anxious child just given his fondest wish. "Of *course*, Ashton, of *course*. Sit. Let's talk."

I told him, "I love your home."

He beamed. "Me, too. Years in the planning. Delighted with it, absolutely delighted. Too large, though, for one old man to rattle around in. I like it filled, like now, filled and overflowing with delightful people and delightful ideas and unknown worlds to conquer. Listen to me, Ashton, nothing else in this old world makes a damn bit of sense. You can take all of your trashy television and your trashy books and shoot 'em off to the moon, for all I care. Too damn much valuable human time spent frittering—yes, frittering. The damnation of mankind is the seduction of pleasure and— seduction of pleasure? Should that be pleasure of seduction? Never mind, same thing, it's all the same thing. Too damn much playing around and not nearly enough—I say, not *nearly* enough dedication to the work."

Well shit, I'd turned him on—the least I could do was sit still and listen.

"Now you take these people, these people here with me, now—and I include you in that, Ashton, you are part of it, now—you people have got spunk. You're building a *world*, you're bringing forth the *dream* from the *crucible*. By *God* I wish I could go back, too, roll back those years and . . ."

Wait a minute! *What the hell was he saying?*

". . . roll up the mental shirtsleeves and by God *make a difference*. That's what I wish, and I envy you, Ashton, I really do."

I had moved to the edge of my chair, one ear turned to that rumbling voice, wondering if I had heard . . .

I said, "Holden . . ."

He held up both hands, turned his head away. "Yes, Ashton, I know, I know. Told you I'm getting senile. You wanted to talk. I gave you an oration. It's just that I get so damned lonely. Even with the house filled with delightful people . . . I get very lonely."

I said, quietly, "That's the human condition, isn't it."

He beamed at me. "You're right. Ever since the expulsion from Eden. Charming allegory. Man coming finally into the awareness of himself. In that awareness, automatically shut off from the rest of nature, from God's protection, cast out. Into the crucible. That's where we are, you know, Ashton. In the goddamned crucible."

I said, "And it gets lonely out there."

"Damn right it does. There are times when I think I will go mad if I do not encounter a truly intelligent, a truly delightful person *right now*—but it passes, it passes, as all things do, it passes."

I quietly suggested, "There's Laura, now, Holden."

He dropped his chin and peered at me from beneath those shaggy eyebrows. "Well, yes, as a matter of fact, I've been meaning to talk to you about that, Ashton." He laughed. "Well, for the past half-hour or so, that is."

I said, "You're a lucky man. She is a beautiful and intelligent woman."

He laughed uproariously. "Too god*damned* intelligent, let me tell you! Yes, I am a lucky man." The eyebrow treatment again. "Of course I would be a *much luckier* man if I was fifty years younger." Still laughing. "Don't know why the hell I couldn't qualify. I've always been a generous man, always worked hard—"

There it was again.

"—never walked on any man's back, but well . . . forgive me, Ashton, self-pity is a cardinal sin, much worse than vanity, isn't it. Forgive me. What were we saying?"

I smiled and said, "Well, you've got your house on the mountain. And Laura. And good friends."

"We were talking about Laura." All sobriety, now. "Ashton . . . ? How do I say this? So that it doesn't sound . . . Ashton, our marriage is a social convenience."

I said, "Aren't they all?"

"No no, I mean that it is *purely* a social convenience. For the both of us. She has her work and I have . . . well, I have mine, and it gets lonely up here. I don't want you to misconstrue . . ." He cleared his throat. "This is very delicate. What I'm trying to say is . . . we don't sleep together. For me, that's okay. For her, terribly unnatural. Get my meaning?"

I nodded assent. "Got you, Holden."

"Fine."

I said, "Well, no, wait a minute. I got you to that point. But I'm not sure . . ."

"Damn it, man, she finds you highly attractive."

I said, "Great. I find her the same way."

"It's a clear field."

I said, "Okay, now I've got you."

He beamed. "Thank you for the nice talk, Ashton. By *God* I enjoyed it."

I said, "So did I. Are we finished?"

He sprang to his feet, said, "Now, the lab."

As we walked away, arm in arm I said to him, "Why wouldn't they qualify you, Holden?"

"Some sort of damned mismatch," he growled. "Nonsense. It's nonsense. I can take it if the rest of them can. Don't I look hale and hearty to you?"

He looked, yes, entirely hale and hearty to me.

But hale and hearty enough to *qualify* for *what*?

The makeshift "lab" had been set up in the basement of the big house and it was now a beehive of activity—scintillating activity, naturally. I had never seen a happier and more co-operative group undertaking. The enthusiasm and obvious commitment was a living atmosphere in there—all, however, with that same sense of excited restraint noted earlier with this group. All wore white lab smocks over blue jeans, some carried clipboards, in small clumps here and there at various instruments and machines—taking readings, comparing notes, the clumps breaking and reforming spontaneously at other instruments with different combinations of players.

It was, yes, a rather breathless atmosphere—heady.

Everyone seemed to notice Holden and me as we wandered through that, acknowledging our presence with a smile and a nod or a wink of the eye, but the activity went right on unchecked as though we were not there, at all. We would pause at a particular "station" and Holden would make a brief comment for my benefit: "Mass spectrometer here, Ashton, they're doing constituency studies"—"Impulse generator, you see, simple Marx circuit, question of mass defect here, I think"—"These fellows are trying a Schrodinger equation on those wave studies"—"Ho, here's the brain of it all, a hundred megabytes computing power in this dandy, Ashton."

They had it all, yeah. And, obviously, the brains to make the most of it.

"How long has this been going on?" I asked my host.

"Oh, quite awhile, yes indeed—one thing, you know, naturally leads to another so we just bring another gadget in. Though I must confess to you, Ashton, I have only the barest surface understanding of what these fellows are up to. They go around with their heads in a cloud much of the time, Lord knows I can't bring them down, wouldn't want to, good Lord no, keep at it, keep at it."

I said, "Keep at what? What are they going for, Holden?"

He gave me an odd look. "Don't you know?"

I told him, "Well not in so many words, no."

"But I thought you'd come to work with them."

I said, "Well, yeah, but . . . I haven't been fully briefed, yet."

He replied, "Well don't look to me for that, Ashton. I'm just the facilities man, here. Ho! Rank amateur! Lord no, don't look to me for that. What's your field, by the way?"

"Psychic phenomena," I told him.

"Ho! There's one for you! *Psychic* phenomena! Bully! *That* is *bully!*"

"Not to be confused with bull*shit*," I muttered.

"How's that?"

"Bully, yes," I said, more clearly.

"How does one go about quantifying psychic phenomena?"

I shrugged and tried a shot in the dark. "It's all one world, Holden."

"Yes?"

"Sure. Question of *field*. Right?"

"Bully!" he fairly shouted. "That is *bully*."

It sure was.

And I felt trapped in his damned crucible.

CHAPTER SIXTEEN
Equation

Notably absent from that beehive of activity in the lab were Jennifer, Laura, and Esau. I asked Holden about that and he rather absently replied that they were probably in the study, his study, which apparently had been temporarily converted into a sort of operations center.

I went looking for that and found it on the main level, occupying nearly half the wing on the north side of the bubble. Very impressive, with heavy furniture and draperies. Two walls were richly paneled; another was solid books from floor to ceiling, featured a ladder on tracks for access to the higher shelves; the other wall was evenly divided between corkboard and blackboard, both very busy. A couple of long library tables and a massive desk were piled with open books and computer printouts. Several smaller tables were arranged in a sort of turret near the blackboard. The blackboard itself was crammed with mathematical hieroglyphics, the tables arranged for studious viewing of such and neatly adorned with ruled tablets and boxes of pencils.

Jennifer Harrel sat at one of those tables, attention riveted to the blackboard, a pencil in her hand toying with a series of equations.

I quietly sat down beside her and inquired, "Have it figured out?"

Without otherwise acknowledging my presence, she replied, barely moving the lips, "A moment, please."

I sat there for about five "moments" before she regretfully put the pencil down and turned to me with a sigh. "Hello, Ashton. Glad to see you're up and about. Feeling okay?"

I had just lit a cigarette. I blew smoke toward the ceiling and told her, "Feeling fine, yeah. Hope I didn't catch you at a critical moment."

She gave me about a one-fourth smile as she replied, "They're all critical now, I'm afraid. Give me one of those, please."

I gave her mine and lit another for myself. She said, "I renounce these damn things fully fifty-two times each year, but every time someone lights one in my presence . . . "

"Addictions are like that," I observed.

She said, thoughtfully, "Yes. What else are you addicted to?"

I shrugged. "Oxygen. Food. Water. Sex. Not necessarily in that order of dependency."

She beautifully arched the eyebrows and said, "Now *there* is an addiction. That last in the order, I mean. But then you qualified that order, didn't you. Let's see . . . where would we rank it?"

I soberly replied, "Sort of floats, I guess. Finds its own order."

She said, "Yes. Well. Other than that, what can I do for you, Ashton?"

That was very definitely a put-down. Or else a kiss-off. I told her, "I was hoping to find Isaac here."

She gave me a rather blank look and inquired, "Why?"

I replied, "Well . . . it's a natural desire, isn't it."

"I don't know. Is it? I find it nowhere in your order of addictions."

"There's more to life than addictions. Is he here?"

"I am not going to reply to that, Ashton."

"Why not? What are you afraid of? I'm on the team, now. Or haven't they told you that. At least, I've been asked to join. I'd like to meet the boss before I decide."

"Who said Isaac is the boss?"

That one gave me a bit of pause. "I naturally assumed . . ."

"Simply because a fuss was raised where you could hear it? I should think—"

"Where the White House could hear it," I corrected her.

"Well now you see, Ashton," she said, with heavy sarcasm, "the White House is not necessarily the very center of the universe. As a matter of fact, my dear, the universe has no center."

"Is that what those equations are telling you?"

"Unfortunately, we have not yet found a coherent solution to the equations."

"Where is Isaac, Jennifer?"

"I am not going to respond to that question, Ashton. Leave Isaac alone."

"Why were you in Los Angeles last Saturday morning? Instead of here, with the team?"

"I am really terribly busy."

"I know that. So why the useless trip to Los Angeles? And why give the entire day over to a . . . ? Jennifer, why did you seduce me?"

She laughed, the nice laugh. "I suppose I did, didn't I."

"Damned right you did. And it has occurred to me that I was set up, coming in. Wasn't I? Did you go to L.A., Jennifer, just to suck me down here?"

She did not reply to that.

"Or, anyway, to establish contact? Did 'the team' retain Greg Souza? And did they do that in the expectation that he would then retain me? Or was it set up like that all the way? Did you people suggest to Souza that—?"

"Why certainly," she said, sarcasm dripping, "and, of course, we had already arranged the murder of Mary Ann Cunningham in time for her corpse to ripen so that you could find it easily, and we hired those men to come to my home after I'd seduced you and sent you on your way so that they could murder me and make you feel obligated at my funeral, and of course we—"

"Huh uh, shame on you, Dr. Harrel, you may not mix the terms of the equation. Two apples and two oranges do not equal four grapefruit. The only solution I am after, in this particular set, is why you happened to be in Los Angeles on Saturday morning."

She rounded up an ashtray, took her time disposing of her cigarette, then told me, in a quietened voice, "Very well, Ashton, I will tell you this much but no more. Please go and play your game of twenty questions with someone who has the time to spare. We knew that Souza had brought in a psychic. We knew—"

"When did you know that?"

"We knew it on Friday evening. He had left a message on my telephone recorder in Glendale requesting a meeting at Griffith, for the purpose of introducing this psychic consultant to the case."

I said, "But he made first contact with me at seven o'clock on Saturday morning."

"That is about the time we confirmed the meeting. You'll need to make your own conclusions from that. I had already returned to Glendale, on another matter. It was felt that one of us should be present at Griffith . . . just in case. So I confirmed the meeting with Souza. That is all. We set nothing up. The sequence of events from that point was purely spontaneous. That it brought you here, and that it led to a finding concerning your extrasensory perception of the energy field was simply fortuitous."

I was not so sure about the "fortuitous" bit, but the rest I could buy, for the moment. It was very like Greg Souza to contact me only after setting it up, first, with everyone else—which could explain the hitman at my driveway within minutes after I knew I was on the case.

Jennifer was saying, "I can understand you being upset with us for knocking you out. But, whether you choose to believe it or not, it was our concern for your safety that led us to that. You see, Laura had already foreseen a possible interaction. When you mentioned a distressing result, she became highly concerned."

"So what did she find?" I asked quietly.

Jennifer's gaze swept the blackboard.

I said, "All that?"

She replied, "Laura's findings have led us to all that."

"What does it mean?" I wondered.

"It *could* mean..."

After a moment, I prodded her with: "Yes?"

"Yes."

"Yes what?"

"You don't get the significance?"

I said, "I don't even get the drift. My math is not that hot, Doc."

"It could have been," she scolded me. "Why in the world didn't you pursue your potential, Ashton?"

I replied, a bit defensively, "Thought I did that. There's more here than math and Bunsens, you know."

She said, "Yes, but... are you aware that you have an impressively high IQ?—I mean, phenomenally high."

I said, "I've always wondered what is really being measured, though. I suspect it does not mean a hell of—"

"Don't be ridiculous! Of course it does! And an obligation goes with such gifts. Some of us are simply born to lead. If we fail to do so, then the lead passes by default to those less qualified. Or less endowed. It *is* an *endowment*, Ashton. And you have tried to abandon yours."

I protested, wryly, "Why do I get the idea that your lecture is serving only to evade a question? What is the significance implied by the equations?"

She stared at me for a thoughtful moment, then: "They are field equations."

I said, "Yes, I gathered that."

"They seek a correspondence between certain aspects of your brain waves and certain aspects of the radiant energy we are encountering here."

I said, "Okay. Any deductions?"

"Several, yes. But without coherence. Laura is now analyzing those in relation to the tissue analysis, hoping to find—"

"Which tissue is that?"

"Nerve tissue."

"Mine?"

"Yes. And—"

"Hold it, hold it. Explain that, please."

"Electron microscope studies. She—"

"Wait right there. Are you talking *brain* tissue? Mine?"

"Yes. She hopes to—"

"Hold it. How'd she get it?"

"She did not *get* it, Ashton," Jennifer explained patiently. "There is no need for alarm, no damage was done, everything was—"

I had been carefully probing my skull with all ten fingers. I told her, a bit testily, "Course not, no damage whatever, just pinch off a little specimen here, a little specimen there . . ."

"There was no specimen work. Esau has developed a technique which allows environmental microscopy at the cellular level without disturbing the host system."

"Then he needs to quickly patent that son of a bitch," I growled. "It would revolutionize medicine. Come on, Jennifer, talk sensibly to me, I know better than this."

I thought that she had been doubletalking me. But maybe not. Her only response to that was a curt, "Perhaps you do not know all that you think you know."

I did not respond to that, because she did not give me the opportunity.

She stood up, showed me her back, and walked out.

Leaving old Ashton with a taste of ashes in the mouth.

I sat there for awhile idly studying the series of equations on the blackboard, even while knowing that I could not pierce that particular veil. I did recognize, here and there, values representing mass and energy, gravity and velocity, in a series which may have had something to do with critical density and the expansion of the universe, but I was just guessing; this stuff was several lifetimes beyond my grasp.

So, what the hell, I'd offended her again—so, why not?— she'd offended the hell out of me, time and again. It was not *her* brain tissue under that microscope! Who the hell did these people think they were?—gods, or something?—that they could just snip off a specimen willy-nilly, without permission . . . ?

I knew what an electron microscope is. I'd seen the damn things. They shot a damned beam of electrons into matter, irradiated the hell out of it, and . . .

Irradiated?

Was not that the very term Jennifer had used in describing . . . ? Yeah. "Palomar Mountain is being irradiated from a point in space . . . "

I went over to the bookshelves to find a dictionary. Wanted to refresh my understanding of *irradiated*. Found the dictionary and found the word though not a lot of comfort from the various definitions, deciding my own understanding was the scientific usage having to do with an energy beam.

But then as I was returning the dictionary to its place on the shelf, my eyes brushed past a slender volume just above it. It was a university press collection of articles on astrophysics by none other than Jennifer Harrel. I pulled it down and leafed through it, found nothing really remarkable.

Then, for some reason, I drifted back to the front matter, found the copyright page, stared at it unbelievingly for a frozen minute or two.

You know how, sometimes, you can get this chill clear through your body, from the top of the head to the soles of the feet and along the branches in between, as though the whole nervous system has become sympathetic to something very strange occurring in the brain?

And something very strange, indeed, was occurring within my brain.

The collection of essays by Dr. Jennifer Harrel had been published twenty-two years earlier.

Which meant that she was somewhere under ten years old at the time. Quite a prodigy. Except that the introduction, by another scholar, spoke glowingly about the good Dr. Harrel's long list of contributions to the world of science, far too many to fit any ten-year span.

I stood right there at the library shelf and read the entire introduction and preface, then I very carefully returned the volume to its place above the *American College Dictionary* and went back to the equations on the blackboard.

I did not know who this lady was. I'd bathed with her, made love with her, spent a delightful day with her. But I did not know who she was. I just knew that she was *not* Dr. Jennifer Harrel.

CHAPTER SEVENTEEN
Ten Big Indians

Well now it was really shot to hell—torn, everything, all of it. Not only was I on a mountaintop with a group of strangers who all could be lying to me; I could not be sure, even, that any of them were who they said they were.

Actually, only three had even come with full names—Jennifer Harrel, Holden and Laura Summerfield. There was at least some evidence—22 years old, but evidence—that there actually was or had been someone named Jennifer Harrel. As to the Summerfields, though... Well, okay, yeah, the custodian over at the observatory—Fred?—had given me a map to the Summerfields' house—so probably there did exist, or had existed, someone named Summerfield.

But how could I be sure about Fred, himself? Or any of those people over there? Hell. I have seen all those movies, same ones you saw, and the things on television, where the aliens quietly slip in and replace all the humans, take their identities, prepare the way for a full-scale invasion from that other galaxy. And there is always a clue, at least one good clue that gives the aliens away. Either they all have four fingers or they can't walk and chew gum and sing "Stars And Stripes Forever" at the same time.

I never saw any in the movies that *scintillated* but that should be as good a clue as any.

I am not saying that this is exactly where I was at, but I was not far away from there. I considered the possibility, soberly, for all of two or three seconds before I began to feel foolish. And yet every other conceivable scenario was even more ridiculous.

See, the problem was one of credibility. Whether we realize it or not, all of us inhabit a very credible reality. We get these very reliable sense perceptions that tell us if we are right-side up or upside down, if we are standing still or moving, if it is night or day, winter or summer. Along with all that, we tend to be more or less gullible. We will take it on faith that the can in our shopping basket is beans and not squash simply because it is labeled beans. And we will drive a hundred miles into the wilderness with no food or water in the car because we believe our gas gauge and the mileage ratings for our car.

We take more of this world on sheer *faith* than most people ever stop to realize.

But then if I get home with the can of beans and it turns out to be squash, which I cannot stomach, I lose a bit of faith. And if I drive out to Death Valley that same day and run out of gas in the midst of desolation, I lose a lot more faith. If no one will stop to lend assistance, when obviously I am going to die out there without help, I lose a hell of a lot of faith—and when I am crawling along the pavement with my tongue dragging in a mirage that has every appearance of cool, clear water—well, yeah, you get the picture, I don't believe anything anymore. This reality has lost credibility for me.

That is where I was at, atop Palomar Mountain that beautiful Monday morning.

I was in an incredible reality.

You see, Jennifer—or the person who was answering to that name—had told me that Saturday on the hillside at Griffith Park that she was the first female in her family ever who had even completed a high-school education, she was the first career woman in the line, and it had been so important for her to make it because everyone in her family was so sure that she was not going to do so. So I could not say to myself, upon finding the 22-year-old publication, that Jennifer was following in the footsteps of her mother or grandmother or whomever—and it would simply be grabbing for too much coincidence to believe there had been an unrelated female astrophysicist with the same name who'd published a book that found its way into this incredible little reality.

No. There comes a time for all of us when we dig in the heels and balk like hell—we will travel no farther along this road—it is the wrong way.

My every action of the previous forty-eight hours had been predicated upon a totally false set of assumptions. First, I had assumed that there was, indeed, a missing scientist whose name was Isaac Donaldson. True or False? At this point, I did not know. I did know that such a scientist had, at one time, lived and worked and published in this country. But I had only Souza's word, and the now highly questionable word of the person calling herself Jennifer, that this scientist was even still alive—and, if so, mysteriously missing from his usual haunts.

Souza himself had only the word of the mysterious entity who had retained him. He had never met Donaldson, had never seen or heard of him until retained to find him.

I had only "Jennifer's" word that the police had ever been involved in any of this or that anyone at all, anywhere, was concerned about any of it—except, again, secondhand from Souza, who spent his whole damned life embroiled in "scenarios," so how could I know how much Souza actually knew about any of this and how much he had dreamed up in his scenario cooker.

True—I had found a dead man outside my house in Malibu. I'd had a run-in with two unknowns in Glendale and another two at Palomar. So *something* was definitely cooking. Again, though, how much of that could have been engineered through nothing more than Souza's blundering about with fanciful scenarios? In the "spook" world, it did not require a hell of a lot of solid intelligence to produce overly-solid reactions.

Suppose, though, that there really was a missing scientist or scientists and that the name of one of them indeed was Donaldson and that everyone in the know in Washington and other world capitals were truly concerned about his disappearance. It did not necessarily follow that these folks atop Palomar Mountain were friends or even allies of the missing man. He sure as hell was nowhere in evidence with that group—and, if he was indeed stashed somewhere in their midst, who was I to believe that these people were protecting him and not, themselves, holding him prisoner for whatever reason?

So the entire thing had lost credibility for me. I knew only that I had met a beautiful lady and made love to her, that I had "rescued" her from an attack in what was purported to be her own home, that she had led me to Palomar Mountain, where I had encountered some strange static on my extrasensory wavelength.

Those were the facts, and they were the only facts I had. It was a hell of a place to be. So I decided to get the hell out.

Prisoner or no, though, I obviously would have to walk out, if out it would be. A truck was pulled in behind the Maserati, totally blocking any exit from the parking space—and, thanks to the two vans hunkered in to either side, I could not even get my doors open to get to my Walther. Two young

Indian men were sweeping the tarmac nearby but would not respond to me in any way. The keys were not in the truck and the transmission was locked, so I could not budge it.

So I figured, okay, and I went back inside to use the telephone but could not get a dial tone to hold long enough to even get the operator.

So I figured, okay, I could hoof it to the national-park campground and find some help there. By now, though, the Indian sweepers had moved to the top of the driveway and had been joined by four more braves with picks over their shoulders. It did not appear that they intended to let me pass— so I figured, okay, what the hell, it could be a long trudge by highway, anyway, so I dived through the bushes and took the fast way down, the very fast way, straight down the mountainside, sliding through shallow snow on the backside. I hit roadway a couple of layers of skin later and kept right on boogying as fast as the feet would move me, even though there was no sign of pursuit.

The long hours on the tennis courts had conditioned me well and I was thankful for it because I was breathing damned hard when I sighted the little market at the crossroads. There was still no evidence that I was being chased so I slowed it down and tucked some breath in, smoothed the hair, shook loose the caked snow that had stuck to my slacks during the downhill slide, and tried to look like any intelligent city fella just out for a stroll along the mountainside in blazer and slacks in the wintertime at five thousand feet.

I certainly was not feeling the cold, and the heated market just about did me in. A customer was engaged in neighborly conversation with the lady I'd spoken with briefly on the way up, Saturday night. Neither paid me any attention. I went straight to the pay phone and used my card to buy a call to Souza. Foster was not going to put me through until he discerned the raw terror in my voice; but there was a brief delay before Souza picked up, and, by this time, the "signs of pursuit" were all too evident and crowding into the market.

I said but two words to Greg Souza which, I hoped, would suffice, given his affinity for the ridiculous. "Code Red," I said, hung it up, and showed a sweet smile to the six braves.

"Ran out of cigarettes," I told them. "Man, I'd slide a mile for a cigarette when the pack is flat."

Not one of them smiled back. I went on to the counter and bought some cigarettes then decided to show some class, went to the cooler and selected a six-pack of Heineken, paid for that, handed it to one of the confused braves, and went outside with them. A pickup truck I'd noticed earlier at Summerfield's was parked there; another one, bearing four more deadpan braves was just pulling in.

I said, "Aw shit, thought I had you guys covered. First there were six, now there are ten. Well, you'll just have to share the damned beer, I'm not buying another damned six-pack."

My humor was lost on these guys, too. I wondered which galaxy they were really from, but not too seriously. Two of them sandwiched me into the cab of the pickup, the other four scrambled onto the bed, and we headed back to Summerfield's—the second truck following closely.

"Thanks for the ride," I said.

"That's okay, thanks for the beer," I said right back to myself.

The guy at the wheel grinned, but very small and very briefly. Now, these guys knew how to be Indians. Shit, they had me convinced.

CHAPTER EIGHTEEN
The Djinn

Esau was seated at the bar in the bubble room, still scintillating but obviously disturbed also, absently holding the telephone handset about six inches from his head and deep in thought. He replaced the handset onto the pedestal as he became aware of my approach, swiveled to greet me with a sober smile.

"Have a refreshing walk?" he inquired.

I had already decided to be cool about the whole thing. "Great," I assured him. "Good air up here."

"Bracing," he suggested.

"Oh, all of that," I said.

I took a stool beside him. He said, "Perhaps we should have our talk now and not wait for dinner."

I said, "Okay."

He said, "Our time grows shorter. I just had a very unsatisfactory conversation with the man in Washington."

I asked him, "Which man is that?"

He chose to ignore the query. "Politicians are entirely too impatient. They tend to demand instant solutions to the most vexing of problems. Ah well." He showed me the charmer smile. "We have less than twenty-four hours to complete the studies."

"And then?" I prompted.

"And then they take us over. It seems that the level of intrigue is approaching critical mass. I feared this would happen. Ever since . . ."

"Ever since I barged in," I guessed.

"Oh . . . no. Don't blame yourself, Ashton." He passed a hand over his face in a weary manner. "We all have known it was just a matter of time."

The guy sure *seemed* sincere. If it was some dumb game being played then he was very good at it.

"At least we are fortunate to be in the United States. Our colleagues on the other side were taken over months ago. Their work has suffered accordingly. Ah well. That says something, does it not, for scientific autonomy. We have been saying for years that science knows no politics. The problem, you see, is to convince the politicians of that."

I commented, "You've been working under a deal with Washington, then."

He smiled wanly as he replied, "More like a standoff. We have been threatening to call in the press unless we get a free hand in this. And, of course, the politicians in power—*all* politicians in power—are dead set against a free press, for all their sanctimonious claptrap about the freedoms."

I asked him, drawn into the "problem" despite myself, "So what does this do to you, now?"

He said, "What it does to us, Ashton, is to impose a near-impossible deadline on our program. We have been working on a crash basis all these months, as it is."

"Are you saying the government will shut you down?"

"What they will do is tantamount to a shutdown. We inhabit a very intolerant age, Ashton. This age, indeed, will no doubt be looked back upon by future historians as the very Age of Intolerance. For this country, anyway. Yet it is all being done under the guise of progress. Progress. What non-sense. We manacle ourselves and call it progress."

I suggested, "A slowdown, maybe. But surely not a shut-down, if what you have here is really . . . "

"Slowdown, shutdown, it's all the same, I fear. How can anyone know how much time we have?" He snapped his fingers. "It came like this." Snapped them again. "It could disappear the same way. It is imperative that we seize the moment. Give the bureaucrats their debating platforms and we shall lose the moment by default. No, Ashton, no. We must push on. We must meet the goal within the next . . . " He consulted his wristwatch. " . . . twenty hours."

"How impossible is that?" I wondered aloud.

"Twenty-four hours ago, I would have said utterly im-possible. Now, however . . . "

"Now, however . . . " I prompted him.

"Well, Ashton, now there is you."

Oh sure, I thought. Now there is another setup. If these guys were playing games . . .

"Which reminds me," I said, suddenly feeling entirely boorish. "Jennifer would have me believe that you have suc-ceeded in invading my brain without dismantling it. Some new technique. Surely she jests."

He laughed softly. "Our understanding seems to be ad-vancing in quantum leaps, since we've begun this . . . Also, of course, we have had the jinn to assist us. So . . . "

I growled, misunderstanding, "Jen?"

He smiled. "Had to call it something." He spelled it for me, then went on to explain: "From the charming Moslem legend. They called them *djinni* or *jinni*. The plural form is *djinn* or *jinn*, whichever spelling you prefer. We settled on *jinn* as both singular and plural. In the legends, the *djinn* are supernatural beings who can take the form of whatever they please—animal, human, whatever—and they can influence human affairs. Seemed highly appropriate to our situation, so . . . jinn."

I said, "Same as genie."

He smiled and replied, "Aladdin and his magic lamp, yes, in which a jinni was held captive through some magic charm and forced to grant the wishes of any mortal who knew the secret of how to invoke his powers."

I asked, musingly, "Could that charming legend be an allegorical truth to some degree?"

All he said was, "That could be said of many of our myths and legends."

I asked, "Do your jinn grant wishes to mortals?"

He smiled slyly as he replied, "It would almost seem so. Of course, we have yet to fully divine the secrets, but I do believe that we are getting closer, much closer. See here, Ashton, there is a very fine—almost an evanescent influence at work here—so fine that it would have gone unnoticed except for a stroke of luck, an almost insignificant perturbation noted within the solar system. We went looking for the cause of that and found the jinn. But the terrestrial influence is just barely detectable using the most sensitive instruments. However, we have developed a method for gathering and refocusing this almost evanescent particle spray, and we have noted some rather spectacular material effects as we refocus into biological target matter."

I said, "I understand that there was some sort of beam covering only the Palomar area, another in the Caucasus mountains of Russia."

"That is true, yes, if you qualify the term *beam* as defining a particle stream within definite boundaries. However, these *beams* are composed of particles at extremely low density. They do not seem to interact with ordinary atmospheric matter in any manner sufficient to announce their presence in our atmosphere. On the other hand . . ."

I said, "That other hand is . . ."

"The nature of the particle itself, the jinn. As I said, hardly any interaction whatever with ordinary matter. With biological matter, however—and, in particular, with nerve tissue—the interaction can be quite spectacular, even in the finely diffused form. The interactive rate is in direct proportion to density, though, which is quite on the low side, so that the effect is rather weak. By refocusing the collective energy and thereby effectively raising the density, then, the interactive rate is naturally increased rather dramatically and so is the effect."

I took a shot. "Your new wrinkle with the electron microscope, then, is . . . "

Esau smiled. "New wrinkle, yes, that is good terminology. Our jinn irradiates the nerve cell *from within the cell itself*. And it emerges in a state which I like to characterize as 'highly colored.' We can read those color bands. They give a rather interesting account of the processes occurring within the cell from which the jinn emerges."

I guessed, "But you could not use this microscopy anywhere except . . . "

He said, "Exactly. At our present level of understanding, we cannot produce these particles ourselves. And, of course, we cannot store the free ones in a box and carry them about with us. We can only refocus what is naturally present and—"

I said, "*Naturally* present?"

He smiled. "Surely you would not wish that I characterize the jinn as *super*naturally present."

"But if the beams are intelligently directed . . . "

"Well," he said, with a look of total dismissal, "there is nothing *un*intelligent about natural processes. Matter of semantics, I trust."

I did not trust that, at all. And my jury was sort of "hung," once again, on the whole matter. But I definitely was wavering, and tilting toward these people, once again. After all, these guys obviously did not intend to blow up the world.

At least not within the next day or two. Surely I could string along for another...

I said to Esau, "There are a number of troubling things on my mind but I guess they can wait, for the moment. I am very disturbed that no one has produced Isaac for my inspection, though obviously he is the center of this program. I am disturbed, also, about Jennifer. There are several questions there. Most notably among them, the book she published twenty-two years ago—at the age, I presume, of eight to ten. And I am disturbed about something I *think* Holden let drop to me in a conversation awhile ago—something to do with wanting to 'go back' somewhere but failing some sort of qualifications. I would like—"

"Dear Holden," Esau said quietly. "The finest man I have ever known, and that needs no qualification whatever. He has been the very soul of generosity and moral support in this endeavor. All our material needs have been met, thanks to him. He has literally spent a huge fortune these past few months, setting us up, providing the necessary tools and equipment. We would have been lost, utterly lost, without him. But, Ashton..."

"Yes?"

"Do not invest undue credulity in anything Holden may say."

I said, "He hasn't slipped that far."

"I'm afraid he has. It is regrettable to see such a fine mind become so disarranged, but it does happen and it has happened to Holden."

I said, "I'll just reserve judgment on that, if you don't mind, along with the other items."

He said, "I can understand why you took your little walk. I just hope you can understand that we desperately need your support, especially now, and that you can understand why we wanted another opportunity to recruit you. I gave the Palas severe instructions that they were not to harm you in any way, nor even to place hands upon you. I trust that they obeyed those instructions."

"Oh sure," I replied breezily. "I even bought them a beer. Why am I so important to you, Esau?"

"We need your gift."

I told him, "I don't use it. It uses me. I can't make it happen. I have failed every scientific test ever devised for me. I can't promise that—"

"We think we know how it uses you, Ashton."

That rocked me back, a bit.

My eyes strayed toward the study as I replied to that. "Is that a 'jinn' equation in there?"

He laughed softly. "Oh yes. And quite a bit more. We just don't have the final solution."

"But you think I can help you get it."

"Yes. We are almost positive about that, now."

"Then why don't you just knock me out again and take it away from me?" I inquired lightly.

He said, "I suppose we deserve that. Again, I apologize, for the team as a whole."

"But you did not answer the question."

"We cannot take it from you, Ashton. We need your active cooperation."

I said, "But something is bothering you about that."

"You are quite perceptive. Yes. Something is bothering me."

"And that is . . . ?"

"There is a certain element of danger involved."

"For me?"

"Yes. For you. Perhaps for all of us."

"Do you want me to invoke the djinn for you, Esau?"

He laughed, but not very convincingly.

And that is precisely what he wanted. Yeah, he wanted that.

CHAPTER NINETEEN
Mutant

I told Esau, "I need to use the telephone."

He said, "Certainly," and slid it toward me.

I called Souza's office and told Foster, "It's Ford. Put Souza on, quick."

Foster replied, "Sorry, sir, he is presently unavailable."

I said, "Foster, you recognize my voice."

"Yes, sir. But Mr. Souza is presently out of reach."

I told him, "Make every effort to reach him. At the very earliest. Tell him the Code Red was a false alarm. Tell me you understand that."

"Yes sir, I understand, the Code Red is a false alarm."

I said, "This is for real, Foster."

"I understand that, sir."

But I had the feeling that he did not. I told him, "I mean that this cancellation is for real. Greg is to undertake no action, repeat *no* action, on my behalf. Tell me that you understand that."

"I understand that, sir. No action on your behalf. I will relay the message at the first opportunity."

I said, "It is very important that you do that."

I hung up and slid the phone back to Esau, smiled, told him, "That's to keep the marines off your back. If I know Souza like I think I know Souza... Pain in the butt, sometimes, but a loyal pain in the butt."

Esau said, "Thank you, Ashton," in that strangely ponderous speech.

The elderly Pala woman brought ham and cheese sandwiches, gelatin desserts, coffee. We had lunch right there at the bar, with very little conversation. Esau seemed absorbed in his own thoughts and I had a few of my own to massage.

It was nearing one o'clock on Monday afternoon when Esau took me to Laura's private lab. It was located in one of the small outbuildings and was outfitted with what appeared to be cryogenic equipment. Cryogenics is, literally, the science of cold temperature phenomena, has to do with the liquefication of gases such as hydrogen and helium, which reach the liquid state at supercold temperatures.

But Laura was not studying cryogenics. Such equipment, here, was utilized purely as a tool for biological experiments. A number of those appeared to be in progress. Fully encapsulated "culture dishes" lined several shelves and overflowed onto a workbench area.

Esau left me at the door and returned to his own work. Laura took my hand with a warm smile and led me to her "bench," sat me down, produced a thick stack of 8×10 glossy photographs, said, humorously, "At least, now, Ashton, you can prove that you have a brain."

I asked her, "Are these pictures of it?"

"Bits and pieces of it, yes," she replied. "Cerebral cortex area."

Before I looked at that, though, I wanted to know about those other "bits and pieces." I was looking at the culture dishes as I asked her, "They are all still inside my head, I hope."

"Be assured of that," she replied soberly. "The culture studies are all done using fetus specimens."

I blinked at that and asked, "Human fetuses?"

"Yes. The mitotics are much more dynamic at that stage of developmenet, so . . ."

I asked her, "Where do you get your specimens?"

"From aborted fetuses, Ashton," she explained, rather brusquely, and quickly moved on to another subject. "Now these photographs are—"

But I was hung up back there with those aborted fetuses. "So you have to be right there Johnny-on-the-spot to get dynamic specimens," I pursued it. "These are living cultures, I take it."

"Yes, of course, we are maintaining and encouraging cell replication and studying the process. But if you mean—no, Ashton, really. *We* are not Johnny-on-the-spot. A commercial lab supplies the flash-frozen specimens. Now these pictures—"

"Somehow that seems downright cold-blooded."

"How else do we progress through science, Ashton?"

I understood the argument. I'd been through it before, inside my own head, many times—not in this particular application but in similar ones—and I'd had to draw certain lines. After all, Dr. Frankenstein had been doing his all for "progress through science." But there were limits, and I'd found mine in lesser trespasses.

Don't get the wrong impression here, though. Laura's laboratory was nothing like Frankenstein's. These were not whole fetuses, not even anything recognizable; it was just a snip here and a snip there, so to speak. Still . . .

"All entirely legal, I'm sure," I growled.

It burned her. "Of course it's entirely legal! What do you suppose we are running, here? My gosh! Use some objectivity, Ashton. It's waste enough that a life is aborted in the first place. Compound that waste by casting the entire effort into a furnace or dissolving it in acid, or whatever they do with the poor things, and—well, thanks, but I like to think I'm doing something more positive than that!"

Our gazes clashed for a long, silent moment, then I shrugged and told her, "Of course it's more positive. So what are you learning?"

She sat down beside me, riffled the stack of photographs, said, very calmly, "We are learning that the life process is far more magical than the cold heart of science would like to admit. We are learning that the organizing processes appear to be obeying a pattern initially established beyond matter and perhaps even beyond the ordinary concepts of space and time."

"What do you mean," I asked musingly, "by *beyond . . . ?*"

"Outside of."

I said, "Sheer energy, then."

She said, "Beyond that, even, as we presently understand the term. Energy can be defined as a certain state of space and time."

"This cannot? This . . . whatever . . . cannot be . . . ?"

"In the ordinary concept, no."

I asked, "What would be an extraordinary concept?"

Laura replied, "It can be hypothesized that the life force, whatever it is, is not indigenous to this universe of space and time."

I chewed that for a moment, then observed, "You know what you are saying, don't you? What you are implying?"

She said, "The implications are rather stupendous, yes."

I said, "You are back to special creation."

"In a manner of speaking, I suppose that could be . . ."

I said, "Hand it to a Billy Sunday and see what he does with it. You are back in *his* camp, now. He will say that he has been telling you this all along. God created the heavens and the earth. Presumably, then, God was somewhere outside the thing being created when he did this. You can't climb into your own test tube, can you. So he created *this* universe and all the things to put inside it. But he was over there, somewhere—outside, somewhere. He created all the living things, saving Adam for last, a special creation into which he blew his own breath, his own very special life force, and put Adam in charge, here."

She said, very quietly, "Yes. I get the picture. But it does not change anything. I have compelling reasons to believe that the life force is not indigenous to this entropic system of expanding space and time."

I pushed the photographs away and told her, "I really do not want to see these, Laura."

She explained, "They are merely microscopic studies of— not actually 'pictures' but representative images of—"

I said, "I know what they are. I don't want to see them."

She showed me a rather bemused smile, said, "A pet superstition, or . . . ?"

"Call it whatever you like," I replied. "I just don't want to become too self-conscious of my mental processes. I have a hard enough time, as it is, trying to . . ."

After a moment, she said, "Please. Trust me not to laugh at you. Stay open with me."

"I'm staying open," I growled. "And you can laugh all you please. I could tell you a thing or two, Dr. Summerfield, about ordinary concepts of space-time. And you'd laugh like hell at me, I'm sure, forgetting that you'd promised not to."

"Why don't you try me," she suggested soberly.

"It's purely an intellectual concept," I growled.

"What is?"

"Space and time. Space-time."

"Oh,"—softly.

"'Oh' is exactly right. We are, all of us, sitting here in the very lap of a mind-blowing phenomenon. It was not mind-blowing before there were minds to blow, but now that man has come into the scene with his oversized brain—and all that mind power—now, suddenly, it's a mind-blower. So we try to limit the size of the explosion. we try to find a handle, a tool of some kind, to de-phenomenize the experience. We intellectualize it. In that effort, we squeeze all the magic out and try to reduce the whole thing to a series of mathematical equations. That is what space-time is, and that is all it is."

"But there *is* an objective world, Ashton."

"Sure there is. And we're trying to understand it. But the world, in itself, is basically incomprehensible. *We* never *touch* that world, Laura, except with the mind. Therefore everything perceived is no more than a mental construct, a mental *specimen*, damn it, of reality. We don't *interact* with this phenomenon. We simply observe it."

She said, after a moment, "You will note that I am not laughing, Ashton."

I said, after another moment, "What have you observed in my brain cells?"

She replied, "In a word, mutations."

"Great. That's really wonderful, Laura. That explains the psychic angle? I'm a mutant?"

"We are all mutants, Ashton. Thank God for that. Otherwise the world would be populated entirely by amoeba."

"So much, then," I said sourly, "for special creation."

"Oh it is still very special," she assured me. "The process involves complementarity, a whole range of it. 'Mutation' is simply a convenient description of the process. One of your 'intellectual constructs,' say."

I said, "Okay. What sort of mutant am I?"

"We're still working on that. One thing is sure, however. Certain neurons of your cerebral cortex have developed receptors which cannot be correlated with what is known about neurotransmitters in the cortex. I characterize these as mutations simply for want of a better name. But there is something decidedly different about your brain, Ashton. And we believe that we know, now, why your brain interacts with the strange energy we have been studying."

I said, "With the jinn."

Her eyes flared and she replied, "You know about that, then."

I said, "Esau told me. He wants me to 'interact' in some controlled manner, I gather."

She replied, eyes downcast, "Yes. We have devised an interesting experiment."

I said, "Esau also told me that there is an element of danger in that experiment."

"I would say, a very small element."

"What kind of danger?"

She raised those dark eyes to mine as she replied, "There is some small concern about the interaction itself. You mentioned the noise, and the dizziness."

"Yes?"

"From just momentary interaction?"

I said, "Momentary, yes, but I wouldn't go so far as to call it an interaction. A perception, maybe."

She said, "With the jinn, Ashton, all perception is interaction."

"How do you know that?"

"All perception, Ashton, is caused by an excitation within certain nerve tissue, produced by an external source."

I said, "Okay."

"Therefore, perception is interaction. The nerve tissue is sampling its environment. It responds within a very narrow range of possibilities, and usually in direct relationship to the nature of the stimulating force."

"Okay."

"You have already interacted with the jinn. Perhaps you have been doing so, in some finer way, throughout your psychic lifetime. This could account for your ability to receive perception without using the five common senses. But this would be a very fine, let me emphasize that, a *particularly* fine, interaction, as compared to the particulate stream now being experienced. In the experiment, moreover, we shall be refocusing that stream into a more concentrated target zone."

"My brain."

"Yes."

"Okay. I'll think about that."

"Another factor should be an important part of your consideration. You have every right to know this."

I said, "Okay."

"It is entirely possible that the differences noted in the neurons of your cortex—remember those?—the mutations?"

I said, "Yes, I remember those."

"It is entirely possible that those almost insignificant differences are a direct result of your presence here at Palomar."

"You mean, I wasn't like that before I came here."

"There is that possibility. Since we have no way to correlate the present findings with what obtained last week or last month or last year . . . well, we can only say, there is that possibility."

I said, "Let me get this straight. You are suggesting the possibility that I have already experienced some mutation as a result of a casual perception—or interaction, as you will—with the jinn."

"You have it straight, Ashton."

I had it "straight," yeah. And I would be straight out of my mind to go along with these people on this thing. Even if I knew who they were or what they were. But I did not know that, even.

But, what the hell, I wasn't here for win or lose. I was here to play the game. And I'd probably found the most exciting game in town.

CHAPTER TWENTY
The Goal

I was not entirely satisfied with my little visit with Laura Summerfield, but she was a very busy lady and I was obviously in the way. In fact, she made it quite clear that I was a distraction, so I got out of there and left her to her work. As I was crossing the yard, I noticed that the Maserati was in the clear. There was a brief debate with my inner self over whether I should or should not seize the moment and get the hell out of there. I lost that one, then lost another regarding the Walther PPK which, I presumed, still nestled in the floorboard compartment.

So I went on to the big house, wondering if I was totally crazy—or totally mutated already and under the control of these people. Hey—if it happens in the movies it can happen anywhere to anybody. I believe the old maxim that anything conceivable is also possible, no matter how far out it may seem at conception. All *science fiction*, I believe, should be regarded as science *future*, because once the concept is there, the reality is not far behind. So don't grin at my state of mind on that Monday afternoon as I was strolling across Summerfield's lawn and forlornly eyeing my Maserati. I wanted out of there, make no mistake about it. With the same mind, though, I knew I had to stay and see it through.

So I lit a cigarette and paused to palaver with a couple of Pala braves. Except that it was sort of a one-way palaver— a monologue, actually. Damn it, I *knew* these guys could speak English. but they concealed that ability very well.

"Hi, guys."

I was not even there.

"Nice day for a slide on the ass down the mountain, eh?"

I was standing where they wanted to work so they just worked around me.

"Running Bear was really a squaw who decided to fuck housework. Or tepee work. Put on this bearskin, see, and proclaimed squaw lib. That's why you guys are out here with the brooms right now."

I could not get a rise out of these guys, although one of them sort of, almost, maybe halfway smiled at his broom. I went on inside, visited the basement and received almost the same treatment down there. That whole team was really pumping adrenaline, now. Godzilla could have walked among them as unnoticed as I.

I kept hoping for a peek, at least, at Isaac Donaldson, but could not even find a clue to his whereabouts. Esau was nowhere in that lab, either—nor was Jennifer. So I went back upstairs and just casually nosed about. It was a hell of a big house. I counted eight bedrooms besides the master suite apparently shared by Holden and Laura, that latter sporting two queen-size beds and two separate baths but rather Spartan in the decor—masculine, I suppose, if you want to gender it—nothing at all like the master suite at Isaac's place in Glendale.

There was also a small maid's apartment and a couple of bunkhouse-looking rooms, a large but entirely functional kitchen—businesslike, no "gourmet" fripperies—a dining hall, and I do mean 'hall,' Holden's study and another, smaller, room next to it which served, I suppose, as the official library. I browsed those bookshelves and was moderately surprised by the range of interests displayed there—everything from the black arts to black holes.

I found the man of the house in the bubble room—or what he called "the club"—idly playing, it seemed, with a small electronic calculator by the window. I helped myself to coffee from a silver service beside him, sat on the floor with my back to the window, tasted the coffee—all without greeting or conversation. He seemed elsewhere.

After a moment, though, he musingly told me, "Make your career in science, Ashton. I made mine in technology. Oh, sure. Very profitable. Indeed. But..." He raised those great eyebrows for a quick scan of the surroundings. "Can't take any of this with me, can I. It's one of the verities, Ashton. We take with us only what we have given away."

"One of the paradoxes, too," I agreed.

Holden was in a mood. He lay down the calculator, took a sip of coffee, hunched forward on the edge of the big leather chair, said, "What's it all about, Ashton?"

I replied, "Damned if I know, Holden. But we're here. Can't argue that."

"Not arguing it. But, damn, I would love to understand why."

I told him, "There was a saying at the academy: ours is not to reason why, ours is but to do or die. Or something like that."

"Cannon fodder," he said.

"Wellll..."

"Certainly. Those who do without reason and die without reason are the unconscious sacrificial victims of those who do not. They are Vachel Lindsay's dumb, blind sheep. And they are led to the slaughter without even knowing that the slaughterhouse was built with them in mind."

In a mood, yeah.

"Have you read Lindsay, Ashton?"

I admitted that I had not.

"American poet. Died in ... thirty-one, I believe. Poet with a social conscience. Can't say that I was with him all the way but—well, you know, Ashton ... right thing can be said for the wrong reason, or in the wrong cause. And vice versa, I suppose. Lindsay was a socialist, I guess." The eyebrows wiggled. "Dirty word, what? He voted that way, on at least one occasion. And he wrote a poem to explain why. Called it, in fact, 'Why I Voted the Socialist Ticket.'"

I tried to get a word in. "Well, politics are—"

"See if I can get it right. These few lines alone justify the man's existence, pay his ticket for taking up room here. Let's see, it goes:

> I am unjust, but I can strive for justice.
> My life's unkind, but I can vote for kindness.
> I, the unloving, say life should be lovely.
> I, that am blind, cry out against my blindness.

"Ho, what about that ticket to immortality?"

I said, quietly, "Bully."

"Bully, yes, damned right it's bully."

I asked him, "What is your life theory, Holden?"

"*Life* theory? Ten words or less, I suppose. Ho. Well, let me see. Can't take it with you?"

I said, "Seriously. And take as many words as you need."

"Ho, yes, I was serious. Serious in reverse, you see. Because you do take it with you. You take all of it with you, Ashton."

"You mean ..."

"Not *this*, no, good lord no, not *this*," he said, with a sweep of the arm. "This worthless collection of atoms and molecules, frozen energy—these are merely the toys with which we placate our restlessness, Ashton. Good lord, who would want to take this trash with him? We do not take the things we build, Ashton. We take the things that build us!"

I said, "Bully."

"*All* of them!"

"Yes?"

"Oh, to be sure! Tear this man apart, Ashton. *This* man, *me*! Describe me without making reference to atoms and molecules."

I replied, very quietly, "Smart. Wise. Beautiful. Good. Generous. Sympathetic. Curious. Kind."

His eyes were watering. He said, "Thank you, but you needn't stick to the virtues. You might also add fearful, doubtful, resentful, self-indulgent, judgmental—oh, the list can go on and on. These are the things that build us, Ashton. Other than atoms and molecules, it is what we are made of. And it is what we take with us."

"Where do we take it, Holden?"

"To the next crucible, I suppose."

"And where is that?"

"Ho! Where *is* that, yes. There's the rub. Where *is* that! I have been peering through telescopes all my life. And let me assure you, my friend, I haven't the foggiest notion where *is* that."

I had a random thought, so voiced it. "This whole universe that is perceptible through your telescopes, Holden..."

"Yes, Ashton?"

"Could be a single culture dish on a very unremarkable shelf in some gigantic but otherwise unremarkable lab, somewhere."

He laughed quietly and replied, "I fear that this is true, in one variation or another, one magnitude or another. But it really does not answer the question, does it."

I said, "Which question is that, Holden?"

"What's it all about?"

I reminded him, "There are very learned people who say it is about nothing at all."

"Claptrap."

"Very learned people."

"We learn what we are prepared to learn, Ashton. Or conditioned to learn. Go looking for an accident, and you'll find one. Search for beauty and you will find that, too."

"What are you searching for, Holden?"

He looked at his hands. "I suppose that I am searching for myself, Ashton."

"Good luck," I said quietly.

"Good luck to you, too, my friend. You must help them, you know, Ashton, you must."

I sighed and said, "Yeah. I'm going to do that, Holden, if I can."

"You can, and you must."

"Why?"

"Don't get you, Ashton."

"Why must I help them?"

He turned those great eyes upon me as he told me, "Because if you do not, they shall never find the most cherished goal."

"Themselves," I decided.

He sighed, and squeezed my arm affectionately. "Exactly, Ashton, exactly."

CHAPTER TWENTY-ONE
The Test

It was a very "interesting" experiment, yes.

Before I tell you about that, though, let me get something into the record, here. I have never been one of that variety of "psychics" who dabble in so-called "spiritualism"—communication with the "dead"—mediumship. I have attended a few seances, out of simple curiosity, and I have known people who claim a close relationship with "spirit guides" who are ever ready to counsel and instruct them. However, since I have also never known anyone whose life situation seemed significantly enhanced through such "contacts," I just really never had a lot of interest in any of it. I mean, I'd never met a "medium" with a Nobel prize or any such measurable recognition for superior knowledge. Most of them I've met, in fact, seem to be singularly unimpressive in any area of knowledge, an observation which has not been deterred by the usual self-serving double-talk and smug mystery with which they would cloak themselves. I figure, hey, you'll know them by their fruits, not by their postures, and I've never seen much of a harvest from those trees.

But, then, what do I know? All of life may be no more

than a posture of one kind or another—and whoever said, in this modern age, that being "fruitful" is what it's all about? Oh sure, "God" said it to "them," back there "in the beginning,"—first chapter of Genesis, predating the later and obviously allegorical account of Adam and Eve and the garden in Eden—"be fruitful and multiply." Never could understand, then, how fruitfulness and multiplication (in the only way possible) became transmuted into the original sin in the Eden account—but then, we humans have never been particularly bothered by religious inconsistencies. In fact, there seems to be a human predilection for inconsistencies, which perhaps explains why some folk take their troubles to "the dead" instead of to certified, living problem-solvers.

But what do I know?

Damned little, as I was about to find out.

I had presumed they were going to set up this thing down in the lab. You know, hook me up, instrument me in some manner or other—do brain waves and all that good stuff while bombarding me with jinn energy.

They did not do that.

They had Palas on the glass roof of the bubble room, cleaning and polishing it—inside, as well, and Esau was up there with them on a makeshift catwalk inside the dome, arm waving the placement of plastic sheets of some kind, about four feet square, in precise patterns. It began to dawn on me, then, that the room was being converted into a massive collection chamber of some sort—literally—a double-convex lens covering the entire room. In a sense, they were building a refracting telescope!

While all that was going on, above, Laura and Jennifer fussed with calculations involving the angle and axis of refraction, plane of refraction and other esoterica, while the rest of the team scrambled about setting up focal lengths, or something, shifting the furniture about, moving stuff in, moving stuff out, trying circles, ellipses, triangles—much ado.

During a pause in the activities, Laura came over to the bar where I'd been trying to remain clear of all that, and asked me, "What do you think?"

I told her, "Best damn furniture movers I ever saw."

"Seriously, Ashton."

"Seriously," I replied, "I feel like you are about to place me in a culture dish."

She laughed throatily, told me, "I'd never do that to you. How could I . . . ?"

"How could you what?"

She slid onto the stool next to mine and leaned close in a conspiratorial huddle. "Do you think," she whispered soberly, "it is possible to love one person and want sex with another?"

I whispered back, "Possible, maybe. Or else . . ."

"Else what?"

"There are a lot of loveless marriages."

"Oh. Okay. Well do you think it is possible to love one person yet find yourself falling in love with another person at the same time?"

I stared at her for a moment then told her, "First, I guess, we must define love."

"Oh that's too damn complicated," she said, frowning at me.

"Let's try something simpler, then," I suggested in my normal voice. "Why do you suppose the jinn shine only on Palomar Mountain and the other place in Russia."

"That is much simpler," she said, hoisting herself upright, then leaning against the bar and fixing me with a disappointed gaze. "They are both very obviously observatory areas."

I said, "So?"

"So what if you were out there somewhere, Ashton, looking down at earth through a very powerful telescope and—"

"How far out there?"

"Not so far that you could not pick out detail with your very powerful telescope. And—"

I suggested, "Make that a microscope."

"For heaven's sake why?"

I said, "Pretend we are in a culture dish. Some gigantic entity is peering down at us through a powerful microscope."

She wet those provocative lips with her tongue and thoughtfully replied, "Okaaay, yes, that's even better. Did you already know what I was going to say, Ashton?"

I said, "Not exactly. I'm still waiting for it."

She smiled and said, "Okay, there's this gigantic entity who—"

I said, "Me, I'm the gigantic entity, and I'm at the microscope."

She was enjoying it. "And as you are examining your culture, you see something that really stands your hairs up. You—"

"I have hair, then."

"Oh, beautiful hair. You see evidence of a strange, unexpected metabolism occurring in your dish. Well, by Jove, there appears to be something *alive* down there."

"And I'm not eating *that* crap."

"*No way* are you eating it. Something very interesting is happening down there. So you increase the magnification and go in for a closer look. Oh, yes, by Jove, *look* at all that *activity*—my God, I believe it's *intelligent* activity because just look at all that *waste* it's throwing up. Isn't this exciting?"

"The joy of discovery," I said, smiling. "So then what do I do? Write a paper on it?"

"Oh, dozens and dozens of papers. And oodles of experiments. And you begin to wonder if you might—just *might*—be able to communicate with your culture. You know, let it know that you're there."

I said, "Yeah, I might try that."

"Sure. And you try everything. But nothing works. It just

goes on its independent way, showing you no attention at all."

"Demoralizing," I said.

"Oh absolutely. So you keep devising new and better ways to get its attention—I mean, you know, without upsetting the dish or—you don't want to actually *interfere*, you just want to establish intelligent contact of some sort. So you finally devise a better microscope, and this baby will resolve infinitely and—"

"Better than an electron microscope, even."

"Sure. After all, Ashton, you are *big*. So you resolve infinitely and you begin searching for some positive, unmistakable sign of intelligent activity. Then one day, lo and behold, right there in your cross-hairs is something absolutely astounding."

"Astounding?"

"Yes. As you are looking down, into this tiny world, you get the very uncomfortable feeling that *something* is looking back at you. Eye to eye, so to speak."

"Eye to eye, eh?"

"Yes. So you resolve the focus a final time and what do you see?"

I said, "Dan Rather."

She punched my arm and squealed, "No, idiot! You see an astronomical observatory. Just like Palomar!"

I said, "And I'm going to *stain* that sucker."

"You bet you are. You're going to mark it and go on looking for other signs. So maybe you only find two that seem significant enough to mark. But, at least, you've got those two."

I said, suddenly very sober, "Is that what we've got here, Laura?"

She was just as sober as she replied, "How the hell can anyone know what we've got here, Ashton?"

"Is that what you expect me to find out?"

"No, of course not."

"What, then?"

"We're shooting in the dark."

"Really?"

"Well . . . in the twilight, anyway. We do have . . . certain expectations. But I can't tell you what those are. That would compromise the experiment."

"You want me to go in dumb and come out smart."

"You could put it that way."

"What if I go in dumb and come out dumber? An idiot, say?"

She showed me a tender smile, said, "Well, Ashton, at least you would be a lovable idiot."

I said, "Lovable or not, I somehow get the feeling that I'll be *going in* an idiot. Do you people really know what you're doing?"

"Not exactly, no. But we have refined our calculations to the closest possible . . . we *think* we know . . . look here, Ashton, we believe that we have ninety-eight chances out of a hundred to find absolutely no effect whatever."

"And the other two chances?"

"Well, one of those . . . we'll all get a lot smarter."

"And the other?"

"Catastrophe," she said quietly.

"So we're going for a hundred to one shot, either way."

She sighed. "Those are the numbers. *Cold* numbers, of course. There is no way to predict the warm numbers."

"What are those?"

"Those are you, my dear."

I said, "*I* am the warm numbers?"

"Yes. The personal equation."

I said, musingly, "How good is Ashton, eh?"

"That," she replied quietly, "is about what it comes down to. Or so it seems. Don't let me set you up for—I mean, if we strike out, don't try to take all the blame onto yourself. After all, we are simply..."

I said, "Just place me in the dish, Laura. Don't worry about it. I'll either see eye to eye with this guy or I'll turn to salt. But does it really matter, in the long course, which way it goes?"

"It could matter," she assured me, dark eyes sweeping me in warm waves. "In infinite ways."

"Then I'll give the old middie try for eye to eye," I told her, sighing. "When do we start?"

"Nightfall," she said. "We want minimum photon interference."

"I'll answer that question for you now," I told her.

"Which one was that?"

"Love. Yes. You can. Love is a restless force. We don't have it. It has us. But it can't have you and me together, Laura. Not because it's wrong but because I'm weak. Too weak to cast off Holden."

"He said he'd spoken to you," she murmured.

"Then tell him that I tried but you changed your mind."

"Why should I tell him that?"

I explained, "I was in a little park last month, close to where I play tennis. Sat down just to enjoy the feel of the place for a minute or two. Little girl of about three came over to me, showed me a butterfly that was resting in the palm of her little hand. It was a very beautiful butterfly. Very beautiful little girl. Obviously delighted with her butterfly. As I was watching, she closed that little hand very tightly and killed the butterfly."

"Oh dear."

"Yeah. Knocked me out. I told her, 'You've killed it, honey. Why did you do that?' She began to cry, wanted me to fix it. I couldn't fix it. Dead is dead, isn't it."

Laura said, "You love your allegories, don't you."

I said to Laura, "Not nearly as much as Holden loves you.

Why would you want to kill that? Or even bruise it? Not with me, kid. I'm too weak for that."

She slid off her stool, patted my elbow, and went back to work.

So. Okay. Better a lovable idiot than . . .

And, of course, I had to stay in condition. For an eye to eye tussle with . . . who?—what? Didn't matter who or what. Mattered only that I knew who I was and where I was.

The rest, I hoped, would take care of the rest.

CHAPTER TWENTY-TWO
Intrusion

There was less than an hour of daylight left and the preparations were proceeding at a feverish pace. The domestic staff had served up sandwiches and coffee for dinner on the run. Various items of heavy equipment, dismantled in the lab, were coming in piece by piece and being reassembled in the bubble.

Esau had just begun an explanation of the alterations to the dome, now completed, and Holden was pacing about with hands behind his back in the midst of activity when something intruded on the beehive.

"You see," Esau was saying, "we don't need the fine imagery required in focusing light rays. We're not trapping visible light. What we are going for here are..."

I thought I knew what we were "going for," there, which is a good thing because the intrusion occurred right there. A rather large helicopter swooped down on us and made a fast pass at about fifty feet above the bubble. I couldn't get a good look at it directly overhead because of the alterations to the dome but I could see it clearly on the downrange, at a distance of maybe a hundred yards, and I could detect no markings—which made me feel pretty good in the initial reaction because my first thought was Souza, and he really had gone for the marines.

But then it did one of those turns that only a helicopter can do, one of those swinging pivots in midair, and came right back at us. I was at the window, by now, and the view was excellent. The chopper executed another swinging pivot and hovered at fifty yards out, maybe a hundred yards up, giving me a beautiful starboard profile.

Shit, it was a gunship, without markings of any kind, and that mother was *armed*. We were sitting ducks in that bubble. I yelled, *"Out! Everyone downstairs! It's an attack!"*

She'd done a right-face in the air and I was looking right up her rockets.

Everyone was just frozen in place, staring with stunned disbelief. I gave Esau a shove and made a grab at Holden just as something sizzling-hot flashed up into my peripheral vision and zipped into that hovering craft.

The flash from the explosion that followed was bright enough to contract my pupils to pinpoints and send dancing lights along my optic nerves but there really was not that much of a blast wave and it was not a total-disintegration type of explosion. The chopper bucked upward and slipped away on its side for several hundred yards, then went down like a rock. *Then* there was a hell of a blast and shit was flying everywhere. It was during this particular moment of observation that I first noted the men up on the drive. One was still down on one knee, a long slender tube balanced on his shoulder. Several others were running toward the house . . . and one of these was Greg Souza.

He'd finally found himself a working scenario, I supposed—and, God, he looked good enough to kiss.

These guys were federal marshals. There were six of them, plus Souza—and one looked an awful lot like Fred, the observatory guy, in different clothing. I had to wonder how many others might look familiar if I'd spent more time at the observatory, but there was little time to wonder about it because they hung around just long enough to make sure that everyone inside was okay, then they took off down the hill toward the crash site, all but Souza.

I overheard Souza tell "Fred" that he, Souza, would "call in the report," so there was more going on, here, than a private eye's response to a friend's "Code Red."

He went to the telephone and spent a couple of minutes on each of two calls, then picked up a dried-out sandwich and munched it as I introduced him to the shaken scientists—all but Jennifer, who walked up and kissed him then ran out with dripping cheeks.

There was still a lot of work to do and not much time left to do it, which Esau apologetically pointed out, so I walked Souza outside for a green-grass conference during which he consumed two more stale sandwiches.

"Nobody," Souza told me, "asked who the bad guys are. Don't they care?"

"They probably know," I replied, "but even if they don't know, I guess there's just not time or interest to worry about it. This is their last night in fairyland."

"Yeh, I know," Souza said.

"You seem to know a hell of a lot for a guy on a retainer," I told him.

He grinned soberly and said, "Don't you want to know who they are? Russkies. All hell has broken loose. Their place over there in the Kazookas, their observatory—"

"Caucasus."

"Yeah, whatever. It blew up, or something—fire, I don't know. Anyway, severely damaged it, killed a bunch of people. We're damn near ready to go to war. They're accusing us of sabotaging their effort. These guys here were a suicide squad.

Been in the country more than month, just waiting orders. Course, we had 'em under surveillance."

I tried to tell him, "My Code Red was a panic error, but I guess—"

"Yeh, shit, I been down here all the time. Took both your calls from down here."

I said, "You set me up, asshole."

"Couldn't think of a better guy," he told me. "They wanted a psychic. They got one. Oh, and listen, don't worry about any stiffs that may be littering the landscape around L.A. That's all been cleaned up, very hush-hush, no need for you to worry about—"

"I did not do it to Gavinsky, Greg."

"Course not. He was there to cover your ass. They got to him. We had a mole. And—"

I said, "Greg, are you telling me that you're still—?"

"I'm telling you nothing and you know nothing."

I was getting burned, again. I said, irritably, "Why the hell didn't you just level with me? That crap about Gavinsky. How'd you know I wouldn't do him?"

"Just wanted to keep you away from home, pal. We had Hank there to backstop it, just in case."

I said, "So you've known the game all the way."

"Hell no. Still don't. Do you?"

I said, "Not yet. But it's getting close."

"Yeh, and I'm damned glad it is, too, let me tell you. This has been a very nervous assignment. My orders are to keep them secure and happy and *no* interference."

I asked him, "How many people do you have on this mountain?"

He said, "Hey, it's not all mine. I just hold the hands. The marshals corralled those two guys you shot up Saturday night. Don't worry, there's plenty of protection. And Pendleton is only thirty air-miles away. I hear they got a helicopter attack-group on alert over there, just in case. This is a hot case you got by the ass, here, pal."

I asked him, "Did Jennifer Harrel know that you are—"

"Naw, naw, I'm just a pain in the ass private eye she had to put up with." He dropped his eyes. "Damn near lost her, didn't I, up there in Glendale. Shit, I had a crew parked right outside her door. Some crew. Those guys didn't even know there was a tussle until you came blasting out of there in your hot rod."

I remembered, yes, a fleeting impression of a presence in the neighborhood. I told him, "Thought I caught a reflection of something up there, yeah."

"Well, listen..." He pulled me a few steps farther from the house. "You need to keep an eye on Dr. Harrel."

I felt something coming and I almost knew what it was going to be. But for some reason, Souza's attitude irritated me. I growled, "Yeah, I'll do that."

He said, "No, really, keep an eye open. Could be dangerous to your health."

"In what way?"

"Either the lady has found herself a fantastic plastic surgeon..."

"Yeah?"

"Or she's a ringer."

Now I was really irritated, despite the fact—or maybe because of the fact—that he'd struck a chord way down in my gut. I guess I attacked him the way I'd been attacking myself. I growled, "That's ridiculous, Greg. She's right here in the bosom of her own science community. Unless you're saying *all* of them are ringers. And what the hell would that buy?"

"All I'm saying," he insisted, "is that she does not check out. Something else. She's been bucking you all the way. Didn't want you into this. Lectured me for five minutes about what she called the *pseudo* sciences while we were waiting for you the other morning."

My irritation was dying under its own weight. I told him, "If she's ringing it, Greg, it's the dumbest ring I've ever heard of. Also there's the matter of—damn!"

He read my mind and said, "The fracas at Glendale? Yeh, I been thinking about that, too. Wondering if she'd staged it just for you. Maybe you barged in at an indelicate time. Could they have heard you coming?"

"Could have *seen* me coming," I told him. "All the way from Catalina."

He said, "Well, it's a worry. Keep it in mind. She'll be taken into custody as our first official act, tomorrow. Then we'll know what—oh, something else. Couple of L.A. cops are sitting back here on the road. Came down to talk to our Dr. Harrel. It's that Cunningham girl."

That one jarred me. I said, "It's making less and less sense, Greg. Are you saying that . . . ?"

"Naw, I'm not saying anything. Just the cops are here and they want an interview. They're about to wrap the case, along with about nine other identicals, and think they have their man. But you know L.A. Very thorough. And apparently there's some little question regarding Cunningham and Harrel. I guess Harrel may have been the last one to see her alive—other than her killer."

I said, "Goddamn it."

He said, "Yeah. Walk up the road with me? Let's try to keep these guys happy awhile longer."

The sun was setting as we took that stroll, and that seemed somehow symbolic of something or other. I was feeling heavy in the heart and leaden in the feet, my thought processes whirling.

Well, after all, it had been a dizzying case right from the beginning. And, it seemed, was getting nothing but dizzier.

The L.A. cops were nice guys. One of them, a Sergeant

Richardson, I knew vaguely from another time. They were understanding and cooperative, and we just stood there beside their car, the four of us, in relaxed conversation. Souza had already done his federal number on them and they understood that something large was on the pike here.

They were given to understand that I was "inside" the case and that Jennifer as well as Professor Donaldson would be available for "an interview" in the early future, although that stuck in my throat somewhat since I had seen no evidence whatever of Donaldson's presence there.

Souza walked me halfway back to the house. As we were parting, he cautioned me again about Jennifer. I assured him that I would keep the eyes open, then I told him that I was getting ready to participate in an experiment with the scientists. I was feeling really ragged, so his response did nothing to help that. "Just hope you know what you're doing, pal. Sounds like the Russkies blew themselves to hell."

I told him, "I haven't the foggiest notion what I'm doing, Greg. Haven't even met this Donaldson, yet. Have you?"

He said, "No, but the way I get it, he talks regularly with Washington by phone."

Jennifer was still in my craw. I said, "Damn it, Greg, how could this woman be anyone *but* who she says. She's been working with these people since . . . since . . ."

He said, "Just since this, I get it. She and Donaldson are the only locals, except for old man Summerfield and his wife."

I asked him, "What do you know about them, Greg?"

He replied, "Not a hell of a lot. Haven't seen the file. He's got a lot of bucks, I know that. Been like a patron of the sciences for quite a few years."

I said, "Maybe there isn't any Donaldson."

"There damn sure *better* be," he growled.

We stared at each other for a moment, then I took a deep

breath and said, "Guess I have to see this through, Greg. Let's just play it where it lays."

He gave a loud sigh and said, "Well, I have the easy part. Just have to keep the lid on for..." He looked at his watch. "...for another fifteen hours. Then this entire mountain becomes a military zone."

I said, "That's what the other side did, isn't it? What did it buy them?"

He replied, "Just tell me if it's really flying saucers. I want to see one."

I chuckled soberly and told him, "So keep your eyes open and your pecker up, pal. You might see most anything. Did you notice what they've done to the bubble?"

Just then Fred hove into view, red of face and huffing with exertion. Souza got the first word in as we turned to greet him. "Check out?" he inquired tersely.

"Not much left to check," the marshal replied. "Major fear now is a forest fire. Crews on the scene, though, so... Did you call it in?"

"Sure I called it in," Souza said. "Just hope you got enough for a positive ID of some kind."

Fred said, "How would we get that, Greg? Even if anything comes through the fire... Want a KGB badge?"

Souza grinned as he replied, "I'd settle for that."

"He'd settle for that, sure," Fred told me with a solemn wink. To Souza: "Forget it, they came to kill and be killed. There'll be nothing in those ashes to deposit on the Kremlin's doorstep." He went on up the drive, halted and turned back to inquire, "Coming?"

"Be right there," Souza replied, then said quietly to Fred's departing back, "To kill and be killed. Crazy world. Crazy." He looked at the domed roof, then said to me, "Damn thing does look like a saucer, don't it."

"It is," I told him.

"What?"

"Well . . . a dish, anyway. Culture dish."

"What's that mean?"

"It means," I replied, "that maybe we have not yet seen the start of crazy."

CHAPTER TWENTY-THREE
Jinnshine

They had an arrangement of concave mirrored surfaces set up in irregular spacing all about the perimeter of that great room. Each was maybe three feet wide and nine feet high, must have been twenty or more of them, mounted via ball sockets onto heavy, wheeled frameworks and controlled from an electronic panel that was located in the bar area. Connecting electric cables snaked all over the floor, apparently to avoid some very precise geometric arrangement of the furniture. A large, heavily upholstered and comfortable looking chair was placed at the precise center of all that; it was presently covered with some sort of plastic sheet that appeared to be coated with a metallic reflecting substance.

I could not help but be struck by the geometric arrangement. My mind leapt back to the browsing at Holden's bookshelves and the presence there of occult books; this arrangement bore a striking resemblance to the sorcerer's magic circle, or mandala, with the round glass walls forming the outer circle and the furniture arrangement serving as geometric designs within the circle. I picked out two sharp equilateral triangles, superimposed in opposition to form a six-pointed star, and there was a "circle within the circle" effect created by a large round plastic sheet—similar to that adorning the central chair—which had been placed over the carpet to cover the center of the room.

I asked Esau, "Where the hell did you guys come up with this arrangement?"

"We are trying," he replied, "for a precise focus. Some minor refinements may be necessary as we go along. We shall have to wait and see."

Wait and see, my ass. I knew what this was. I said, "Why don't you just ask Merlin about that?"

He gave me a patient smile and replied, "I am still having difficulty with you, Ashton. I never know when you are joking."

I told him, "It is not now, Esau."

He took a long, exaggerated look about the room, then said, "Yes, I suppose I see what you mean."

"It's a mandala," I said accusingly.

"The universe is a mandala," he replied musingly. "Something in the subconscious, perhaps, that—Jung thought so. Tried some mandala therapy on some of his patients, I do believe. Churchmen must have divined something there, too, though probably in the wrong spirit." He laughed. "Did you catch me there?"

I had to grin. "Caught you, yeah. You're getting downright sophisticated, Esau."

He was very pleased with that comment. "It's true, just the same. The stained glass of cathedrals are rampant with mandala geometry."

I said, "So are the rituals of Hindus and Buddhists. But—"

"It's universal," he said, closing the discussion and moving away to help position another piece of equipment.

Universal, yeah, I told myself, but how did it get into the subconscious in the first place? *Who told* all those geeks and gooks and priests and ordinary people who see them in their dreams that this particular geometry holds some sort of universal significance?

Anyone in recorded times who'd ever tried a bit of black magic had tried it in a circle just such as this one. Witch priests and priestesses to this very day do their numbers in such circles, perform ritualistic sexual acts in there, invoke charms and spirits and magical feats in there. Eastern mystics meditate and levitate and oscillate in there, African witch doctors draw them in the dust with a stick and commune with the spirits in there.

Now these guys, these space-age creation physicists, expected me to invoke the jinn in there.

So, okay. I would try to do that.

"It begins," Esau announced calmly, and gave a nod to the guy at the control panel.

The computer-driven concave mirrors at the perimeter began their weird, undulating rhythm—almost a "scooping" motion into the atmosphere of the big room. Several other instruments, the function of which I had absolutely no notion, began a low, droning hum.

I was seated in the central chair, with the metallic sheeting beneath me, both in the chair and at my feet. Laura and Jennifer sat to my right and left, respectively, their chairs positioned slightly to the rear and angled toward mine. Esau sat facing me from a low couch, about six feet away, Holden beside him. Except for the guy at the panel, the others were scattered about in what appeared to be a random pattern but which actually formed the geometric configuration noted above, all facing me and more scintillating than ever.

The guy at the panel was softly calling out numerical values at roughly ten-second intervals. After about a minute of that, Esau asked me, "Are you getting anything, Ashton?"

I was "getting" something, yeah. A slow-motion *deja vu*

tingle, beginning low in the spine and spreading upward, the kind that usually gives you a sudden shiver but this one was even shivering in slow motion.

I reported to Esau, "Something, yeah. Moving up the spine. A sort of shiver."

He looked elated but the voice was calm and controlled as he instructed me, "It's a controlled interaction. I *knew* it. Try to cooperate. Don't fight it."

And Laura's voice, at my right ear: "Try to relax and invite it in, Ashton. If you get disturbing static, try to hold through it, see if it will subside."

I was beginning to get "static," yeah, plenty of it—except that it really did not sound like static after the first burst, more like a cacophony of discordant voices all sounding at once, like in a crowded bar during happy hour with all that shrieking and babbling...

The guy at the panel was still announcing numbers but his voice began to sound like an anesthetist's as he's counting you down to dreamland, growing fainter and more distorted moment by moment.

I heard Esau gasp and call my name, repeated several times, but I just did not feel like responding, and I heard him say, to someone, "He's all right, he's through it," but I didn't know what the hell I was "through" and I did not care.

It was the quickest drunk I'd ever known—and I've tried a few of those in my time. I was soaring, feeling no pain whatever—feeling, actually, sublime or exalted or whatever it is when you're just ecstatic all over—post-orgasmic ecstasy, maybe, relieved and happy and fearless and warm and good.

And I was light, I had no weight, I was in zero-gravity and free-floating. But I could examine that intellectually, as though it were happening to someone else, and I could marvel at it and wonder what was next.

And the *wondering* seemed to produce a whole new train

of phenomena. I rushed through some sort of brightly colored vortex in which was spinning with me all the things I'd ever done and dreamed of doing, all the things I'd ever seen or wanted to see—and shit I heard music, the most beautiful damned music, and I was directing the Boston Pops through *Scheherazade*—yet with all of this, at the same time marveling at it and trying to intellectually process it, I was aware also that I was talking a streak, in mathematical symbols and equations.

I would hear Esau's voice: "Wait, give that again, was that E to the minus tenth?"

I would be processing that while not really caring if I answered him or not, all the while knowing also that I did not know how to respond even while hearing my voice respond, "E to the minus tenth *squared*," or some such; I don't know now what the hell I was saying.

At the same time, and in the same mental space, I was getting screwed out of my brains by forty beautiful women—no, really, precisely *forty* and all at the same time—while simultaneously pursuing a deeply meaningful dialogue with none other than Socrates, in *his tongue*, no less.

I could even marvel at the psychedelic patterns and wonder how many of my neurons were firing all at once at a given time, and I remember trying to calculate how many could fire at once without destroying the brain.

I had never experimented with mind-altering drugs but I have read accounts by others who have, and I would have to say that my experience with the jinn was similar. With an important difference, however. I have never known of anyone who came back from a chemical "trip" with any truly new or revolutionary idea or concept, or with any hard knowledge they had not gone in with. Apparently I had, if the reaction of these theoretical physicists is a measure.

I was coming down, or coming out or back or whatever, and knew it—and suddenly "knew" that I knew a lot of stuff

I had not known before. The talking was done and I was like stretching out across an open doorway, with one foot in one room and the other foot in another room and just sort of stuck there between the rooms. I could hear the excited voices around me and I could see—as though across a great distance—Esau leaning toward me from his couch with both hands extended, trying to quieten the reaction in there, and I could hear him more clearly than I had ever heard a human voice before as he tried to restore order.

"Please, please! I believe there's more! Do you have more for us, Ashton?"

I did, indeed. I had a P.S. And though I did not now what it meant, I knew who it was for.

"For Holden," I said, hearing my own voice from a great distance and peering across a great yawning void into those dancing eyes next to Esau's. "Zero, plus or minus zero, equals zero. One plus one equals infinity."

Then I moved on through that doorway and immediately felt like death warmed over. I had an incredible headache all over my body, if you can imagine that, and I was certain that if I dared breathe I was going to begin throwing up and never, ever stop.

But I heard the old man's, "Bully, bully!" just as I crossed another threshold and fell into merciful unconsciousness.

I took something else across that threshold, also, and it is well that I did not dream. Because I took with me a new knowingness, a new understanding and appreciation of the dizzying events of the past few days.

I truly "knew" Esau and Jennifer and Laura and especially Holden—and I understood the secret that bound them together with the other scientists in that room.

I understood their studies, their anxieties, their mission.

And I knew a deep, almost essential sadness as I moved across that welcome threshold from pain to oblivion . . . because I "knew," also, where these "studies" would take them.

CHAPTER TWENTY-FOUR
Whatever

I awoke on the same hospital bed in which I'd awakened earlier that day—though fully clothed this time, except for shoes, and covered with a light blanket. Holden sat at the foot of the bed, grinning and wiggling eyebrows at me. Laura stood beside me. Apparently she had just drawn a blood sample. A sleeve of my shirt was folded up to the elbow and a small Band-Aid was stuck to the arm. I felt okay but not superb, exactly—a bit fluttery, maybe, but no real discomfort.

Laura showed me a sober smile and inquired, "How do you feel, Ashton?"

I told her how I felt but the voice did not sound much like mine. Throat was raspy, dry. I sat up and drank some water. It helped. I asked, "How'd the experiment go?"

"The experiment," Laura replied, "was smashing. Positively smashing." She laid me down again. "Stay there until I get back."

She departed. Holden stayed, regarding me with absolute delight. "Dear, dear Ashton," he murmured.

I said, "Went okay, huh?"

He semaphored with the eyebrows as he replied, "Okay enough, dear Ashton, that our learned colleagues were sent scurrying back to their math models bursting with exciting new concepts. The general consensus, it would seem, is that we are at the edge of a breakthrough which is—well, I would say, at the very least, as profound as the movement from classical to quantum physics."

"Something new under the sun, eh?" I commented tiredly.

"Ho, yes, very good, I would say so. Yes."

"How long have I been out?"

"No more than—well, I would say under a half hour. Had us worried for a moment, there, my boy. Looked dead." He shuddered. "Lord, maybe you were. Do you remember any of it?"

"Some, yeah, but not . . ."

"Do you recall, dear Ashton, leaning forward and fixing me with a blazing gaze and speaking directly at me?"

The blazing gaze, no, but I remembered the message for Holden, though not in total coherence. I said, "The sum of . . ."

"No no, not—here, it's burned into my ears. Let me— zero, plus or minus zero, equals zero. One plus one equals infinity. Ho! Bully!"

I felt weak, a bit disoriented. "What does it mean, Holden?"

"Why Ashton! It's the qualifier!"

"Fancy that," I said, and went back to sleep.

I dreamed, this time, and Holden was clad in a wizard's robes and a conical hat. He was performing magical rites at a blackboard except that the mystical symbols were algebraic and his helpers were positioning and repositioning blocks of equations, stacking them all around the blackboard. A flying saucer with brilliantly flashing lights swooped down to hover above the blackboard, then the saucer dissolved and became a transparent holographic image in the colors of the rainbow then turned into a rainbow and Jennifer was walking down it, naked and glistening, and she was carrying my head under one arm and shouting instructions to the wizard's helpers. Then, shit, she turned into Dorothy and my head was Toto, and I knew in a brilliant rush of insight that Holden was really the Wizard of Oz and all of us were trying like crazy to send Dorothy home. I was filled with anxiety because the tornado was approaching and Aunty Em was worried about Dorothy; we had to get her back before Em discovered she was missing. Then Esau showed up, drifting across the whole scene on a magic carpet made of goatskins and I *knew* in another insighted flash that he *really was* Jacob but where the hell was father Isaac? Esau/Jacob did a swinging pivot with his goatskin carpet and cocked it at the blackboard. The wizard looked up at him and bellowed *"Bully, bully"* but I was looking straight up into the carpet's rocketry and I knew it was not so bully. They fired, but the firing was like neuronal bursts and the rockets themselves were flashing across synaptic gaps and diffusing rapidly. They hit the blackboard as words which replaced the wizard's equations and, as the smoke cleared, I could read the words blazing at me from the blackboard.

> *unto every one that hath*
> *shall be given,*
> *and he shall have abundance;*
> *but from him that hath not*
> *shall be taken away*
> *even that which he hath*

I said, "What the hell does it mean, Holden?"
"It's the qualifier," said the wizard.
I don't know if we got Dorothy back in time or not because I woke up, then, on my side and peering crosswise into Jennifer's eyes at a distance of about two inches. She was kneeling beside the bed and resting her chin on my pillow,

eyeing me with loving concern. I jerked away from that close engagement in a reflex motion. That startled her and she reacted backward, also, then recovered with a smile and said, "It's just me. Are you nice, very nice?"

I believed I was. At any rate, I felt much better than before. I told her, "My kingdom for a cigarette."

She wrinkled her nose and said, "Those things will kill us, Ashton."

"Fat chance," I replied. "They'll have to stand in line."

She laughed the good laugh and found my cigarettes on the table, lit two, handed me one, deposited an ashtray between us on the bed. "This brings warm memories," she said quietly. "Seems so long ago. So much has happened."

I sucked greedily on the cigarette before I responded to that, released the smoke as I said, "The universe is a mandala, or so Esau told me."

"Meaning . . . ?"

"What goes around, comes around, I guess. But it has been nice, very nice, most of it. It's about over, though, isn't it."

She dropped her eyes, sighed as she replied, "I guess it is. Curious thing about . . ."

"What?" I prompted her, after a moment of silence.

"The exclusivity of experience, I guess."

"How is it exclusive?"

She delicately shrugged. "It's a singularity, isn't it. We simply cannot be all things at all times."

"Like . . ."

She smiled sadly. "Like doctor, nurse, Indian chief."

"Rich man, poor man, beggar-man, thief, eh?"

"Right. We can't be all those at once, can we."

"Not sure I'd want to be," I decided.

"In a different time and circumstance, Ashton . . ."

"Yes?"

"I could be madly in love with you, you know."

"Thanks," I said soberly. "But then, you're wearing that ring, and..."

"That's what I meant."

"Yeah."

"You have been, uh, rather undecided about me, haven't you."

"Right up until the séance," I replied, "yes, I have."

"The what?"

"Séance. That's what it was, you know. By any other name..."

She smiled and said, "A rose is still a rose. Yes. Maybe you're right."

I said, "Sure I'm right. The wizard's circle, the whole bit. How did those old guys *know* that, Jen? Is there anything essentially incomparable between the magician's symbols and the mathematician's symbols? Isn't it all gibberish to the untrained mind?"

She said, "Yes, you're right."

"It is said that even Solomon had his symbols and gibberish through which he invoked magical powers."

"I hadn't heard that."

"Sure. But what if it wasn't gibberish, and what if the symbols carried mathematical significance?"

"Yes, you're right." She paused. "Ashton..."

"Still here, kid."

"I don't... quite know... how to tell you this. You see, I..."

"Don't have to tell me," I said. "Already know. And it's nice, very nice."

"I've had to lie a lot. Even passively."

I said, "It's okay."

"You already know about...? Isaac? The rollback?"

She saw the answer in my eyes.

"Who told you? When?"

"No one told me," I assured her. "I got it in there."

"In where?"

"The magic circle."

"You mean . . . ?"

"Yeah. How long was I in there?"

"The productive period was eight minutes and seventeen seconds. We have it on tape, all of it, no garbles. But how did you—?"

"All math?"

"Yes. An entirely new model. Almost a new language. We've had to set up analogs. Ashton, you could *not* have gotten that from our equations, not even if you understood them. And you told me this morning that they were beyond you. Yet your new model not only provides those solutions but posits a whole train of others. Do you understand what you've done?"

I said, "I don't even know what I've done. Anyway, I didn't do it, it did me. And it did me, also, an understanding of what this is all about. Not in math, though, in essential knowingness. Do you understand that?"

"Not exactly."

I tried to explain. "It's like . . . I *know* what you know, the same as if I am working from your memory pool. In that same way, I know what Esau knows and what Holden knows and—but maybe with no more understanding, but I know what you think you know."

She replied, struggling with that, "Then it is conceivable that your new model is merely an induction from our own . . . feeble . . . a combining of all the minds into a single organism of reason—my God, the empirical data pool would be . . ."

"Mind-blowing, yeah," I said, "and I think it damned near blew mine apart."

"And that could be the explanation for—the jinn could simply be—I mean, in the fine, neuronal interaction . . ."

I said, "An inductor, yeah." But it was purely a shot in the dark, almost an automatic response.

She leapt to her feet, said, "My Gosh! I have to get this to . . ."

I told her, "Include Holden."

"Yes, I—he thinks—"

"Give him the benefit of any doubt," I suggested. "It couldn't matter that much now, to him, anyway. He's going to get there one way or another, and soon. Give him a shot at this way."

Her eyes were sparkling—no, scintillating—with excitement. She ran to the door, turned back to blow me a kiss and say, "Ashton . . . thank you."

"For what?"

"For not hating me."

"How could I hate a nice kid like you?"

How could I, indeed? I knew her like I knew myself. No, better than that. I knew her like I *wished* I knew myself.

It is said by virtually all the mystics that good and evil are mere states of mind—that is, human constructs. God, or the eternal being by whatever name, does not recognize the difference because the difference does not exist, cannot exist, in unity.

And the more enlightened of the mystics have gone on to point out that there is not, and cannot be, a duality in unity. All is one and one is all. That includes you and me, kid, and the rabbit and the snake—the butterfly in the little girl's hand as well as the hand, itself, kings and slaves, cabbages and stars.

Where do those old guys *get* that kind of thinking?

Maybe my "shot in the dark" to Jennifer, that automatic response, was pretty close to the mark, at that.

How does all this *stuff* exist independently yet come together as a unity?

Maybe, yeah, maybe the jinn was the grand inductor. It

had sure inducted the hell out of *these* people. In physiology, an inductor produces a change or a response in an organism.

Grand Inductor. Yeah, maybe so. Another term for *whatever*.

CHAPTER TWENTY-FIVE
Eternally

The case was getting "curioser and curioser," as you will see. But let me try to develop some analogy to help you understand where we are, now. If you go to a movie tonight, you may be able to relate the most memorable scenes, or at least the central theme, of that movie to a friend a few hours later, or tomorrow at work. You will not, however, have total recall of every scene, every word of dialogue, unless you are most unusual. By next week you will recall even less of the movie and next year you may have trouble "remembering" if you even saw that particular movie.

A lot of the same sort of thing occurs routinely with all our experiences. We may "remember" tonight that we bumped into an old acquaintance this morning but already not be sure as to where the meeting occurred or what exactly was said. The next time we bump into that same person, we may have difficulty remembering when we saw him last.

This is all very useful and practical, for all the value placed on "good memory," and there is evidence to suggest that the human brain is designed to function in just this manner. Recent research suggests that the brain has some method to automatically sort and file experience in what is termed a "print" to either a short term or a long term memory, depending upon the importance of the experience. Presumably "short term" memory decays quickly and is lost forever, in this theory. However, I have seen remarkable recall of trivial detail by hypnotized persons, so I am not comfortable with this quick-decay idea. Maybe there is a passover to a dead storage file—to all practical purposes, lost, but indelibly woven in somewhere and accessible by extraordinary means.

Any way you look at it, though, the human brain is a wondrous device. I am told that it may contain as many as one hundred billion cells, or neurons, with a complexity that defies all attempts to fully understand how it works. So don't get too tough on me for shooting in the dark here. I'm no oracle and certainly no authority on any of this stuff.

And that is precisely the point I am trying to make. For all the apparent wizardry unleashed in the magic circle, I am still just a guy with an ordinary brain and subject to all its limitations and programmed functions. Through some "magic," I was able to briefly link up with some other ordinary human brains to effect a sort of "brain bank"— like combining data pools in a computer link. But I did not "become" all those people. For awhile—a very brief while, as it turned out—I had access to an abundance of strong memory prints, and apparently there was a brief integration of all that in my own mind, an integration which produced some rather remarkable intellectual conclusions. One minute later, however, or one second later, for that matter, I could not repeat any of those equations and had only the vaguest "memory" of having uttered them in the first place.

In that same sense, then, my "merging" of consciousness with all those others did not automatically absorb any of the personalities into mine. When I say that I "knew" something about that personality, I speak of general assumptions, an integrated impression or hunch or understanding involving the totality of personality but not the trivia underlying that totality. It is a bit more complicated than that, because there are various plateaus of "totality," but this is basically where I was at, that night on Palomar Mountain.

I "knew" certain things about these people without truly understanding the detail that formed such knowingness.

Like, I know that Gary Cooper was the good guy in *High Noon* without really remembering all the detail of characterization that led to that generalization; and I recall the character with fondness, remember that he was a lawman of some sort, and identify with the central theme of the story but I cannot now recall a single line of dialogue from that movie.

This is about where I was "at" with Jennifer, Laura, Esau, Holden, and the others.

It was a marvelous place to be, let me assure you. I was awed, almost overwhelmed, by the tiny grain of understanding I had of these people—and there was enough of know-ingness there to send my own mind into a spin if I thought about it too carefully. But it is so damned far out, all of it, that I have this problem, now, of how to present it to you in a credible way. If I just lay it out for you the way it was laid out in my mind at the time, you are probably going to be skeptical as hell, as well you should be. So I have to beg your indulgence while I set it up properly and give you the opportunity to come at it through some of the detail that formed my understanding.

So back to the story.

I must have been really beat up because I drifted back into sleep soon after Jennifer left my room, that evening, and this time I guess I really made it count because it was past midnight when I again awakened. I think I must have dreamed the whole time. You will fully appreciate that only if you understand something about modern sleep research.

The sleep labs have discovered definite cyclic patterns in the sleep process, varying between periods of deep sleep, during which the brain produces an EEG pattern termed "synchronous," characteristic of mental inactivity; and periods of light, or REM, sleep with a desynchronized EEG pattern more characteristic of the waking, or mentally alert, state. Dreams supposedly occur only during REM sleep; presumably REM (Rapid Eye Movement) always indicates that the sleeper is dreaming.

The average adult spends about twenty percent of sleep in REM, with the first REM stage occurring after the first hour of deep sleep, lasting for about ten minutes that first time but with the REM stages lengthening to about an hour as the cycles continue. Infants appear to spend about half of their sleepy time in REM, and no one really knows why this is so, but it makes me wonder about my own maturity because I believe I do most of my sleeping in the alert REM state. I can even doze off for twenty seconds in the middle of the day and get a dream out of it.

Incidentally, for all the sleep lab-research, nobody really knows why we dream or what it means to dream (let alone what dreams, themselves, mean) but there are a lot of learned theories on the subject. The theory I personally prefer—for ordinary, run of the mill dreaming—has a dream as nothing more remarkable than the spin-off result of the brain's data-processing activities while we sleep; that is, the brain is going through the day's activities, sorting and filing and throwing out the debris.

It is fairly obvious, though, to any unbiased researcher, that not all dreams are of the "run of the mill" variety. Some of the greatest music and the noblest ideas ever to grace our planet were conceived in dreams. There is also an unmistakably indismissable psychic component to some dreams. And then there are those dreams that almost certainly seem to originate in some other reality; we classify these as mystic dreams, and human history in every culture about the globe has been beatified by such dreams.

I do not know how to classify my continuous-REM sleep on that Monday evening atop Palomar Mountain. I do know that I fell asleep exhausted, experienced some five to six hours of extremely active mental alertness while asleep, and awakened totally refreshed. I felt, in every sense, a new man. Perhaps I even scintillated, for awhile there. And I believe that I perhaps threw off a lot of "debris" during that period.

Anyway, I came out of it tingling with the vague memories of what I'd experienced earlier that evening and an even more vague understanding of it. I ate the fruit I'd stashed earlier that day, washed up, and went adventuring again.

This time I went straight to the dining hall. I had noticed a collection of portraits adorning those walls on my first casual inspection but had not given them any particular attention. These were photographs, not paintings, but done up in heavy frames and mounted similar to paintings, large—about 11 x 17. Holden was there, and looked about the same as in the flesh, so I presumed the others were relatively recent, too.

Holden was there, yeah, and in favored company. To one side of him was a man of roughly the same age who looked, yes, like Dr. Zorba—Isaac. I studied that one closely, and had to smile. How relatively slight are surface signs of age, yet how dramatically amplified are those subtle changes in our gross perceptions. A line here, a puff there, a bit less hair or a bit finer and less pigmented, a slight droop as flesh succumbs to the law of gravity; a map of experience: that is what age is, yes, and I smiled at the Edwardian texture of this map.

Are you Esau, or are you Jacob?

He was neither, both sons of the biblical Isaac, but he was Isaac himself—right under my nose all the while yet invisible in the mask of youth, scintillating under the onslaught of a fantastic infusion of "living wave" energy.

Tingle? Bet your ass, tingle. Every hair on my body must have been standing at attention as the physical evidence in those portraits confirmed the vague understanding I'd gained in my tussle with the jinn. Not just the evidence itself but the implications—my God, the implications! Who would not "scintillate" under the influence of such an organic "inductor" and who would not be bursting to tell the world of such magic? The evidence before me answered a lot of questions, yet the tingling spoke not of answers but of a whole trembling train of new questions.

Jennifer and Laura did little to relieve that tingle.

Jennifer was dignified, almost stately, heavy silver hair upswept from the graceful curve of a still beautiful neck, eyes that still mocked with the constant threat of warmth—still beautiful in a way that stole over you—Bergman, yes, as Golda Meir, and I was in love with her.

Laura was an ancient Pala woman who had learned the white man's ways early, mastered them, blended them with herself behind thick eyeglasses resulting from too many years at the microscope—the long hair a bit coarser, now, and less defined as to color—but beautiful, yes, in her way, still very beautiful.

They all were there, all this incredible team of senior scientists, the "young" scintillators who had edged my perceptions with visions of aliens from faraway places; they were indeed aliens, of a sort, from as far away as Ponce de Leon and his fountain of youth and who knows how much farther, into the myths and fables and longings of every generation of man since Adam, from all the mandalas of all the wizards in all the lands who patiently practiced their incantations and recited their magical equations—good lord of all the lords, how long and how diligently had mankind searched for this tingle which now leapt at me from these photographs in reverse chronology—and how very privileged I felt to be able to see the past as future.

Or to see, perhaps, the past and future as a continuum with the present. That, you know, is what eternity is. And eternity, I believe, is what these people had unlocked.

CHAPTER TWENTY-SIX
Decision

I found the team in the study. They had moved in two computer terminals and printers and the place showed evidence of recent bedlam. All was quiet now, though, peace reigned, and the human atmosphere in there was one of sober reflection.

Holden looked up as I entered and motioned me toward a chair at the blackboard turret, where he sat with Laura and Jennifer. Esau/Isaac was toying with some expressions on the blackboard while conversing in a monotone with another scientist.

I waded through discarded printouts and joined the group at the table. Holden showed me a delighted smile but said nothing. The two women looked beat, barely acknowledged my presence.

I observed, to no one in particular, "Looks like it's been back to the drawing board, eh?"

Jennifer replied, in a weary voice, "Back and back and back again, yes."

Holden, energetic as ever but speaking in a stage whisper, said, "But they've deciphered it, by God!"

"Doesn't appear to be a particularly happy conclusion," I said, glancing around at the sober faces in that room.

Laura smiled faintly and replied, "Not necessarily unhappy, though. Just, uh, sobering."

I said, "I see that, yeah."

Jennifer said, tiredly, "May I have a cigarette, Ashton?"

I passed one to her, lit it, said, "What's the conclusion?"

She got the smoke going, then replied, "You don't want that in twenty-five words, I hope."

I told her, "I'd settle for one or two."

"That's easy, then," she said. "In a word, *life*."

"Life?" I echoed.

Laura picked it up, very soberly. "The jinn are life."

I looked at Holden and said, "Okay, I'll take those other twenty-four words."

He waggled the eyebrows and replied, "Let Laura do it. It's her field."

"Some field I picked," she said, with a grim smile. "Doesn't even belong to our universe, it appears."

"Ho, we're all aliens," Holden commented.

"Is that the conclusion?" I wondered.

Laura said, "It is the inevitable result of our conclusions."

I said, perhaps in an incredulous tone, "Now wait a minute..."

Jennifer shot me an oblique gaze. "We've all had the same reaction, Ashton." She sighed. "Ego problem, I fear. Certainly we should have been prepared for it, though. The pointers have been there, all along."

I said, "I just don't get the graveyard atmosphere in here. If you people have the solution then it is a triumph of science. So where are all the triumphant scientists?"

Holden said, "Ho, my sentiments exactly. She said ego problem, though, and there's your clue, Ashton. See here, these people have immersed their very lifetimes in the study of this universe as the home of mankind. Now they've discovered it's only a blasted *way station*, so to speak. Put yourself in their place, my boy. Way you do that, way I did it, was to imagine myself the only self-aware ant in the colony. Oh, say, how puffed up I am, how delighted with my own brilliance after I have deduced all the secrets of the anthill. Then, one adventurous night, I crawl out onto the face of the planet and behold the lights of the city. In a sudden intuitive flash, I divine a whole new order of anthills and an intelligence so far surpassing my own that I am abysmally humbled with awe. And I don't know whether I should venture out into that magical night with all its unknown perils or if I should very quietly retreat into my own hill and pull the hole in behind me."

Laura was giving him a warm gaze as he spoke. When he finished, she said, "Very *good*, Holden."

Jennifer sighed and said, "Yes, Holden has it by the balls. Just wish I could..."

Holden waggled eyebrows at me and said, delightedly, "She's been so horny since she rolled back."

"Haven't we all," Laura said, but without humor. "And now it seems..."

Something was wrong, here. Holden's analogy may have been right on the mark and perhaps partly responsible for the mood of the group, but there was more to it than that—quite a bit more, I decided.

Before I could get an angle on the thought, though, Esau/ Isaac stepped over from the blackboard and extended his hand to me.

I shook it, asked him with a smile, "Are you Esau or are you Isaac?"

He smiled back as he replied, "Isaac, of course. Regret the little charade, Ashton. Jen told us that you were familiar with some of my work." He ran a hand across his face. "Didn't want to shock you too much with this, uh, anomaly. Remarkable thing, isn't it."

I replied, "Remarkable is an understatement. I was just down in the dining hall, checking out the portraits."

He smiled. "Yes, well..." His gesture included everyone present. "You see what has happened."

"I see," I said, "but I really do not understand."

"Nor did we, at first. Had us completely fooled. Thought the jinn were interacting biologically, at the cellular level—but good Lord—it was happening too fast. A biological inductance was perfectly understandable, yes—even a rapid effect, locally, as any other spontaneous mutation—but broadcast uniformly throughout the organism? Good lord!—we had a tiger by the tail and we knew it. Then Laura showed us that the interaction was not biological."

I said, "So you were using yourselves as guinea pigs."

"Unwittingly, yes, at first. Didn't know what we were involved with there, you see. We had noted what appeared to be biological interaction. We were doing focus studies, similar but much less concentrated than last night's experiment, using tissue specimens. Noted some small effect on the specimens, enough to enormously mislead us for awhile. But then we began to experience the changes within ourselves. Then, yes, conscious guinea pigs. And you see the result before you."

I gazed at Holden and said, "But..."

"But, yes, isn't it so often the way...? Our greatest friend and most generous benefactor experienced a negative effect early on. We very regretfully were forced to exclude him from—"

"Ho, made me senile, you see!" Holden rumbled from the sidelines.

Isaac smiled at him and said, "Senility is reversible, Holden, you know that. At any rate, I'll take you senile over twenty ordinary men at their best." He turned back to me. "We know better, now, thanks to you and your postscript for Holden."

I said, "I remember that but it hardly seems earth-shattering."

"Ho!" said Holden.

Isaac smiled at him and said to me, "A philosophical postscript, perhaps, but it has led us to a reassessment of the data and a better understanding of Holden's negative reaction."

"The negative has become a positive!" Holden said delightedly.

Laura took his hand and declared, "And we're going to take care of this mismatch, aren't we."

He said, "Bully, ho, bully!" and tears sprang to his eyes.

Jennifer surged to her feet and strode away, left the room.

Isaac watched until she was entirely out of sight, then observed, "She is deeply troubled."

I asked the obvious question. "About what?"

He replied, "About the jinn. What it means. Where it is taking us."

I said, quietly, "You *know* where it is taking you, Isaac."

He said, as quietly, "Yes. We do, now. And that is the problem."

"Do we," Holden rumbled, "pull the hole back into our anthill? Or do we venture into the great unknown?"

Isaac said, "He means that quite literally. And we must make the decision very quickly, while the option is still there."

I gazed about the quietened room and decided, "But you've already made that decision, haven't you."

He gave me a warm smile and an affectionate pat on the shoulder and replied, "To use your terminology, Ashton, the decision has made us."

I could see that. Yes. I could see it all around that quietened room.

CHAPTER TWENTY-SEVEN
Turnabout

I went looking for Jennifer and found her in the great room, at the window, staring into the night. The scene was exactly as I had last seen it—the geometric designs, the equipment still in place.

I went up behind her and touched her lightly on the shoulder with my lips. She shivered and said, "Bet you can't guess what I was just thinking about."

I told her, "Turn off the jinn and I'll give it a shot."

"I have been very frightened of you, you know."

"Shouldn't be. I seldom ever leave teeth marks."

"Worse than that, my love. You leave worse than that."

I said, "But that's not why you ran from me at Malibu."

"No. That was a challenge."

"It was?"

"Yes." Our eyes were meeting in the reflective surface of the window. "I decided if you were genuine then you'd find us. If not . . . who needed you."

I said, "Cold. That is very cold, Jen."

"I needed you, genuine or not. Still do. But, then, your authenticity has been resoundingly established, hasn't it."

"Has it?"

"Yes. You have the jinn."

"Or they have me."

She shivered. "It seems they have us all." Hollow laugh. "Difference between thee and me, my love—you've always known it. Pardon me if it takes me awhile to get used to the idea."

I pointed out, "By whatever name, you know, it's the same force. Same result."

"For you, maybe. Not for me."

"Why not?"

She turned and presented herself to me in a fashion model's pose. "What do you see, Ashton? A mature woman with one foot into her sixties? Hardly! But that Hale seduction story I confided to you happened *thirty years* ago. You were a mere child, yourself, at the time. My God, Ashton, I was twenty-seven years old and still a virgin! Bride of science, indeed! Well, I'm fifty-seven now and a virgin still, to all practical purposes. Never married, never bore a child, never loved a man so much that it made me ache inside."

I said, "I understand."

"Do you? How could you possibly understand? Wait thirty years, Ashton, then look back and tell me that you understand. How could you possibly understand?"

I shrugged, smiled, and said, "So, maybe I don't."

"No, maybe you don't. This is not a cosmetic job I'm wearing, you know. I'm ovulating again. I am at the very peak of life again. I have a second chance at it. Can you understand that? A second chance! I can do it all again! But, this time, with the benefit of mature viewpoint."

"I think that's great," I told her. "So why all the agonizing . . . ?"

"Oh damn it, Ashton, you know I can't do it again!"

"Why not?"

She turned back to the window, brooding darkly onto the

night. After a moment, she quietly declared, "This all means something, doesn't it. It has very deep meaning."

"Life's like that," I said.

"I mean . . ."

"I know what you mean. What you need to understand, though, is that nothing has changed, not really. Your perceptions may have changed. But the thing being perceived has not changed. Which reality do you want, Jen? Do you want the aching love, the house full of kids? Nothing wrong with that. Take it. And feel blessed. But don't feel damned by any alternative. Take what you need, Jen. Because what you need needs you, also."

"That is very profound, Ashton."

"It's just that kind of world, Jennifer."

She said, "Thank you. I love you. I could be your mother. But I love you."

She was not looking at me, though, not even at my reflection. Her arms were crossed at her chest, feet wide apart, head bent.

I told her, "That's the sweetest thing one person can say to another," and then I got away from there and left her to her own thoughts.

The timing was pretty good on that, too, because Greg Souza was at the front door. He pulled me outside, then into a car, saying, "Damn, it gets cold up here at night."

We lit cigarettes, cracked a window for ventilating the smoke. I asked him, "What's up?"

"Time," he replied.

"What does that mean?"

"I owe you this, because of—and don't ever say that I don't pay my bills. It's no breach, anyway, because I got this indirectly."

"So tell me what you got, Greg."

"This old Indian mission down. here at the foot of the mountain . . ."

"Yeah?"

"It is now a staging area. Soldiers and equipment all over the place."

I said, "Okay. Is this a rerun, Greg? Didn't you already tell me they're declaring a military zone?"

"Yeh. But I told you eight o'clock."

"So now what are you telling me?"

He consulted his wrist, said, "It is now five minutes past two. In fifty-five minutes, a big government jet will land at the air base up by Riverside. It will disgorge a large contingent of civilian and military scientists, whose mission is to lock up everything here—I mean *seal* it—audit and pack up all the data that has been developed by Donaldson's team, and haul the whole thing back to Washington for analysis—Donaldson and his people included."

I said, "They'll have a hell of a time packing up the jinn."

He said, "The what?"

"Private joke," I said. "I take it our scientists have no vote in the matter."

"You take it right. No more vote than any other draftee."

"Like that, eh?"

"Yeh, exactly like that. And they're not waiting for eight o'clock. They'll be coming here by choppers from Riverside. Soooo...I figure, what with the usual milling around and all on the ground at Riverside, maybe an hour. They could be here by four. So if you would like to avoid all that..."

I said, "They'd take me, too?"

"Hey, you're on *my* list, pal. But who's to say what they'll think if they find you cozying up, here. They might decide to just, uh, what the hell, debrief you too."

I said, "Okay. Thanks, Greg."

"I'll be right out here somewhere. Keeping things in sight. You know. So, when you're ready...Just present yourself. I'll come collect you."

"I'll want my car."

"Give me the keys. I'll move it. I have a hunch nothing will move out of that gate after these guys arrive. Pentagon bunch. You know them."

Yes, I knew them. Had been one myself, once, as had Souza. We both knew them.

I gave him the keys and told him, "Be gentle, please."

He chuckled. "Yeh, I know, she bruises easy."

I told him, "We were wrong about Jennifer Harrel, though."

"Yeh?"

"Yeah. It will seem crazy but it's not. She's who she says she is. And I'm not so sure I want to miss any of this, Greg. I want to see some Pentagon faces when they know what I know."

"What is this you know?"

I gave him a long look, then told him, "Naw, naw, you'd never believe it."

"Hey, come on, don't do this to me, Ash."

But I was doing it to him. And happily. I stepped out of the car and closed the door tightly behind me.

Everyone, now and then, has to pay his tab. Scenario Souza was now even.

CHAPTER TWENTY-EIGHT
Jinnesis

I had better explain a couple of things before you get the idea I'm doing to you what I did to Souza. What exactly are the jinn and what kind of bull is this about the fountain of youth and all that.

Let me assure you, first, that it's no bull. These people were actually "rolled back" in biological time to a moment when their *élan*, or life force, was at its most vigorous. But note that I said "biological" time, not calendrical. They did not lose the years, or the experience, or anything whatever in real time. What they lost was biological decay.

How account for that?

Well, I am shooting in the dark again—and this is no easy explanation, at best. It has to do with what life really is and what a living cell really is and how life itself asserts domain in an entropic reality. If that sounds like double-talk, I'm sorry. I will try to make the talk as singular as possible... but you will have to bear with me, once again, while I discuss these very singular ideas.

First of all, etropy. The word was coined by a nineteenth-century German physicist, man named Clausius, to describe a thermodynamic principle in nature: the observation that a certain amount of energy is unavailable for useful work in any system undergoing change. The universe itself is such a system, and it has been postulated and experimentally demonstrated that entropy (disorder; useless work) always increases and available energy always diminishes at a steady rate in our physical reality. What this means, essentially, is that our universe is steadily decaying and has been doing so since the big bang which supposedly began our race through space and time. There will come a time when it all runs down, when there is no further energy available for useful work—such as star-building and the formation of dynamic matter. Our *entropic reality*, then, is a dying universe in which the natural tendency is toward further and further disorder.

Upon this scene strides man, carried on the back of countless generations of other life forms from the amoeba to protoman. The miracle of life is that it is here, at all. Life gathers together, unto itself, the energetic particles of a decaying universe and infuses them with purposeful activity. That is a powerful idea. Even the lowly amoeba is a majestic miracle of purposeful activity when considered in company with a band of lifeless molecules. The molecules are steadily decaying and giving up energy while the amoeba absorbs that energy and grows with it.

Still with me?

Consider, then, that the amoeba is built of essentially the same particles of matter that build the lifeless molecules. They all started together in a star, somewhere, the erupting product of nuclear fusion and the building of complicated atoms, flung out into cold black space to drift and coagulate into congealing lumps of matter which somehow in time found a space for itself in orbit around the star that built it—and the same debris that built the decaying molecular planet built also in its dust—or vapors, whatever pleases most—a vehicle by which quite another force, not encountered in any free form anywhere in creation, began purposeful activity.

That is what life is. And that is how, to the best of human understanding, life began on this planet.

That understanding, however, is woefully inadequate at the present stage to answer the deeper questions about life. It does not answer, nor attempt to answer, even, the question of how "purposeful activity" arose in a lump of lifeless matter. Most scientists today would avoid the question by saying it is not in the province of science to answer such questions. That is pure bullshit. It most definitely is within the purvey and the province of science to ask as well as to answer every question bearing on the nature of this reality we all inhabit. So don't let them get away with that.

One scientist who did not try to get away with it was the guy I mentioned earlier, the late astrophysicist Gustaf Stromberg. It is a pity that this man did not have access to recent findings in the still-infant science of microbiology. The postulates he did come up with, while microbiology was still a primitive science, would have been Nobel material had he not been so far ahead of his time. As it was, he was largely ignored or pooh-poohed by his contemporaries, who perhaps were embarrassed by this scientific lapse into what surely was regarded as mysticism.

Well, maybe that isn't fair. Einstein himself wrote a glowing cover blurb for one of Stromberg's books, *The Soul of the Universe*, in which he sets forth a brilliant theory of life processes.

Stromberg, you see, though an astrophysicist, apparently became intrigued by what was happening in microbiology during the second quarter of this century. And he was fascinated by the research being done into basic life processes, particularly that having to do with the embryonic development of a living creature, or embryogenesis. Considerable spadework had already been done by various eminent biologists, including De Beer and Huxley, to show that embryonic development occurs within an "organizing field," and the German biologist Gurwitsch had published a study in 1922 in which he stated, "The place of the embryonal formative process is a field (in the usage of the physicists) the boundaries of which, in general, do not coincide with those of the embryo but surpass them. Embryogenesis, in other words, comes to pass inside of the field. What is given to us as a living system would consist of the visible embryo (or egg, respectively) and a field. The question is how the field itself evolves during the development of the embryo."

Which brings us full circle back to the jinn.

Gurwitsch's "field" (in the usage of the physicists) is an electromagnetic field and it posits the existence of "an organizing field" of electromagnetic energy in which the embryo is embedded.

Stromberg envisioned "living wave systems" which he christened—are you ready for this?—*genii*. It is patently unfair to do so, but I will try to sum up, for quick consumption here, Stromberg's conclusions by quoting a single paragraph from his book, *Soul of the Universe*:

> "Matter and life and consciousness have their 'roots' in a world beyond space and time. They emerge into the physical world at certain well-defined points or sources from which they expand in the form of guiding fields with space and time properties. Some of the sources can be identified with material particles, and others with the living elements responsible for organization and purposeful activities. Some of them exist in our brain as neurons, and some of them have a very intimate and special association with their ultimate origin. They are the roots of our consciousness and the sources of all our knowledge."

Mr. Stromberg was describing, I believe, the jinn, although his own terminology was *genii*.

I also believe, however, that Stromberg's *genii* were in a high degree of organization, since he was speaking of embryonic life fields, which would presuppose greatly specialized and sophisticated living systems.

Our jinn are not quite in that category, as you shall see.

CHAPTER TWENTY-NINE
The Adventure Begins

The cleanup had begun, in the study. Isaac was erasing the chalk marks from the blackboard. Others were rounding up computer prints and stuffing them into boxes which, in turn, were being carried away by Pala braves. Books were being carefully returned to library shelves. Holden stood to one side, absently watching the activity, now and then leaping to assist a Pala position a heavy box in his arms.

I watched Holden for a few minutes, wondering about that delighted and delightful old man and trying to picture him as he would have looked fifty years earlier, decided he was a hell of a man at any age.

Funny, you know, how you can project a "process" forward or backward in time and still identify the result of it. Life appears to be a process. A process of *what*, I can't say—but it seems that all of us begin as a gleam in our father's eye and then something inexorable takes over to project us into the matrices of space-time and then to keep us moving through a flow of experience from which we may never withdraw until it is time to escape space-time. That which occurs between gleam and withdrawal is a process of some sort, meaningful work lending itself to purposeful activity in a process conceived by a far greater intelligence than mine.

Holden had said that we take it with us, all of it—and I was wondering what it was that he would be taking with him, what net result of his own personal processing. Suppose that he was bringing it to me and that I existed in that other world, somewhere outside space and time: what would be the gift from Holden that could be built nowhere but here? Joy, perhaps, delight, a rare appreciation for experiential magic, a sense of generosity, a sense of purpose, a sense of . . .

Yes, *senses* of things, not the things themselves.

So . . . was that what "life" was processing? If life had come to the space-time universe to find something of value which could not be built in that other universe, could *sensory experience* be what it is all about? And what *was* being built behind the matrices from these space-time processes? What would Holden bring as a gift of value to that endeavor? He'd called this earth a *crucible*. So what had he built, here, of his own life processes, for that other world?

I was just wondering, with no expectation of finding an answer. But maybe I found one, just the same. Because when Holden spotted me standing there, and turned to me with that delighted grin and hurried to me with that boundless enthusiasm—at the age of seventy-five, no less—I found myself responding in kind and I knew what it was that men like Holden build for that other world. And, yes, in his case, one plus one most certainly equals infinity. If I ran that other world, I would not shut this fellow down, not ever.

"The adventure begins, Ashton," he announced with a delighted shuffle of eyebrows.

It had begun quite a bit earlier, for me, and I was not sure I could take much more, but I told him, "That's bully."

"Yes, damn right it's bully." He hugged me and I hugged him back without a trace of embarrassment. "See here, my friend," he said, after the embrace, "I have been authorized to invite you to stay with us. It was a unanimous vote. We'd all like you to be one of us."

I said, "I already feel that I am one of you, Holden. But I appreciate the gesture."

"It's no gesture, my boy. Let me assure you, it's no gesture. And our adventure is just beginning. We'd like you to share that with us, if that is your desire. No pressure, of course, ho!—no!—no pressure of any kind, not in a matter such as this!—but—"

I said, "I don't have a lot of rollback available, Holden. If you could bottle a few jinn for me, though, why I'd be delighted to take a rollback or two home with me for future use."

He laughed and I laughed and we had a good time with it while he explained that was not exactly what he'd had in mind; then Isaac came over and the whole thing turned very sober again.

"The troops are coming," I told him, then went on to relate what I'd learned from Souza.

The news did not particularly surprise him. "Perfectly understandable," was his comment. "Actually they have been very patient with us. Much more so than..."

I knew what he meant. I said, "It was a disaster over there."

He nodded and replied, "Yes, I got that from Washington yesterday morning. And I can understand their concern that this thing be approached with full safeguards. However..."

I said, "You know what the pressures will be, I'm sure. They'll want to put you people in test tubes and probe for every conceivable effect. And they'll want to draw more blood than your bodies are capable of producing. They'll be trying to synthesize and package this thing, and I would suppose the first move would be toward establishing a brain bank—politicians first, no doubt—to preserve senior wisdom. You people are going to be first-line curiosities. If

Barnum were alive today, he'd be lobbying for the exploitation rights." I was beginning to feel like Scenario Souza, but Isaac came to the rescue.

"We have considered all that, of course," he told me, "and it has helped form our decision. Do you know what that is?"

I knew what it was, yes. I'd known it hours earlier, back in the circle, before any talk of "decision." But it was not all that clear a knowingness, more a vague premonition or *a priori* reasoning to an inevitable effect.

"Essentially, yes," I replied. "I know what you must do."

"Good." He looked to Holden, back to me. "Will you join us?"

I said, very quietly, "Not this time, Isaac."

"I understand," he said. "You have worlds of your own to conquer, first, what?"

I said, "Something like that, yes."

We shook hands, and then we embraced. There were tears in his eyes. He said, "God bless you, Ashton."

"He blessed me with you, Isaac," I replied. "And Holden, and all the others. Tell him, when you see him, that I told you that."

He smiled a smile of pure delight, turned it onto Holden, then the two old friends bade me farewell and went arm in arm into the great room.

Laura had been waiting her chance at me. She, too, embraced me, and very warmly. I kissed her lightly on the lips and she gave me a moist nibble then laughed softly and said, "I hope you understand."

I replied, "Of course I understand. Some things I don't, though."

"Such as?"

"The rollback itself."

She said, "Well, don't feel bad. It had us going for awhile, there, too. We were trying to ascribe it to a chemical reaction, some hormonal effect at the cellular level. Very dynamic process, you see. It took your insights to make us see that the process was occurring at a much more fundamental level."

"Which is?"

She laughed again and told me, "You already have the answer to that."

"I do?"

"You gave it to us."

I said, "But I have a lousy memory."

She laughed some more—obviously very happy, at this moment in time—then said, "There isn't time now, my dear, to refresh your lousy memory but I'm sure it will all come back to you, bit by bit. You will awaken in the middle of some night, I'm sure, and cry out 'Eureka!' And then you will understand how space-time structures are vested with living energy from outside space and time to expand within space and time in thermal equilibrium."

"You are speaking of an energy packet," I decided.

"Of a type, yes. The space-time structure that arises is a direct consequence of the energy initially vested in a living field. This structure imbeds itself in matter as a guiding-wave structure to harmonize with spatial properties, expending its own vested energy in the process. As the initial living energy is dissipated, the guiding waves are proportionately weakened and the material structure suffers consequent destabilization. This is the phenomenon we observe as the aging process. It is not a strictly biological process, as classical theory supposes, but is a consequence of entropy."

I said, "Really."

"Yes. Well, to qualify that, entropic influences within the living system which are then broadcast throughout the biological structure."

I said, "So the rollback results from an increase of energy in the living field."

"A shot in the arm, so to speak, yes. The jinn revitalize the living system."

"Which, I suppose, are jinn, itself."

"Jinn systems," she corrected me.

"Got you," I said, but I was not sure of that. I would have to think about it. Even then, probably, I would never be sure.

I told her, "Godspeed, Laura."

She told me, "Speed as relative to what?"—laughed softly, pinched my cheek, and left me standing there with forty billion questions trembling at my tongue.

The adventure, yes, for these people, was just beginning.

CHAPTER THIRTY
Eye to Eye

For all my spouting on the subject, I know nothing of life and death, birth to burial and all that comes between. I am an observer and know it, but know not what I observe nor even where I stand for point of view.

I began this case in one of those unnerving confrontations with brutal death and I am still aware of the bruises placed upon my senses by that confrontation, but I am no closer to an understanding of any world in which such ignoble trespasses occur as a matter of routine. I am aware of and immersed in the human longing for justice and beauty and compassion, and all the transmutations thereof as viewed in our institutions and philosophies, so I cannot turn blindly and mutely away from human suffering with trite phrases to appease the pain, and yet I know that the brutalities and the ugliness and the pain inherent in our human situation is not the true story of mankind, is not the moving force that propels us from amoeba to starman—but also do I stand dumb and frozen in the apprehension of that force, unable to comprehend or to even intelligently examine its face or its implications.

So that is where I was, on that Tuesday morning atop Mount Palomar, as my new friends made final preparations for the greatest adventure of all. Isaac had hit it squarely on the head in his observation, moments earlier, that I would not join them in the adventure because I had my "own worlds to conquer." All of my worlds are within myself, and I had conquered none of them. How would I then dare to venture into a greater unknown, unsure as I was of the most intimate unknowns?

I could not go with them, no, but I must admit that I greatly would like to have done so. I felt a deep sadness, also, with the realization that the time for the great farewell had arrived. I had developed a strong affection for these hardy souls, despite the brief time I'd known with them, so it was an especially emotional moment when Holden came back to me in the "safe zone" to take my hand once again in a private good-bye.

"Wouldn't be here, except for you, you know," he reminded me, the strong old voice thick with emotion. "You are a remarkable young man. See to it that you stay that way. Do not surrender to frittery. Keep the horizons distant."

I replied, "Thank you, Holden. Come back to see me, from time to time, why don't you. Keep me straight. The door is always open, you know."

He said, "Ho, yes, that would be bully. Very well. I shall try to arrange that."

And then there was Jennifer again.

She told me, "I think I just may find the time to do it all. What do you think of that?"

I told her, "Eternity is a very long time. So why not?"

She kissed me, passionately, said, "I'm going to do this again someday, too. With you."

I said, "Maybe you will, kid. I hope you do."

"You're still calling me 'kid.' That's sweet."

I said, "Are we talking biological age or what?"

She said, brightly, "You're right. Maybe you're old enough, somewhere, to be my great-great-grandfather."

I told her, "I think it's more likely that we all began together, in that 'somewhere,' where time and age are meaningless."

She arched her brows at me and said, "Give me time to think about that, eh?"

"Take all the time in the world, kid," I told her. "You've got it."

And then, finally, there was Isaac.

I asked him, "Are you Esau? Or are you Jacob?"

He laughed dryly as he replied, "Delighted that you read the old accounts, Ashton. Keep doing so. Much wisdom there, if one can find the key. Take that very story, now..."

I wondered, "Who told it first?"

He suggested, "In your terminology, perhaps it told itself."

"I like that, yeah," I decided.

"All the records are in the lab, Ashton. We've combined them all into a commentary. I doubt that much can be done with them, without the jinn, but..."

I said, "Well, it will keep the boys busy for a long time, anyway. Maybe it will even inspire some new mandala theory and a new age of wizardry."

He sighed. "At least there will be no jinn bombs. I jest, of course."

I said, "Yes, I caught you there, Isaac."

He went away smiling, and that is my final memory of Isaac.

It was twenty minutes before four o'clock on Tuesday morning, Palomar Mountain time, when they all took their places in the circle. Several new items of instrumentation had been added to the equipment. The control panel was preset with an automatic timer and I had been cautioned to remain in the safety zone behind the bar. There was no light in there, now, except that provided by the starry night, but I could see them clearly, all of them, and I could even hear their excited breathing.

But then the machinery started.

I was staring so intently into that twilit room, for what seemed an interminable period, but later turned out to be a matter of some thirty seconds, that I began to wonder if my eyes were playing tricks.

I could see movement, in there—or I guess you could call it movement, some fine disarrangement of the molecular atmosphere, and this movement was infused with a pale glow of color. I wondered if that same effect had been present when I was in that circle during the earlier "experiment" or if this was a new wrinkle produced by the added instruments. I would want a shot at those records in the lab but doubted very much that I would ever see them. And I wondered if I were seeing the jinn or the jinn effect—like a bubble chamber—or if my eyes were just playing tricks.

But then I saw Holden lean forward in his chair and swivel that beautiful old head toward me. He was glowing, and I mean literally. As bad as the lighting was, I could have counted the hairs of his brows, and I knew that he was looking me straight in the eye.

Something happened there, in that eye contact. Something ignited inside my own head and I had the sensation of peering out through a telescope—or maybe it was down through a microscope—infinity is infinity, isn't it, from whichever end—I just know that I was looking into an entirely different reality, and I was seeing it through that eye-to-eye contact with Holden.

It was a brief glimpse, the flash of a shutter and then it was gone, and I realized that although I seemed to be looking through Holden I was no longer looking *at* Holden. That is, not the *physical* Holden. I blinked, and in that blink the whole thing resolved and I could see the physical Holden in his chair, head swiveled for eye contact with me, and I saw also another Holden, an ephemeral Holden shimmering against the window glass some ten to twelve feet above the physical Holden, a rapidly shrinking holographic image of Holden.

This was all very quick, hardly more than a finger-snap in time, yet I saw it clearly. The holographic image, or whatever, contracted to a point then flared up again and expanded instantly into an almost fearsome sight. The closest thing to which I can relate this second image are drawings I have seen of the human nervous system—the nerve trunks, themselves, streaming down from the brain, and of course the brain itself. Then, much quicker than I can tell it, here, that second image convoluted into a small standing wave of sheer energy, contracted to a point, and vanished.

I said, or something inside of me cried out, "Ho! bully!"— but already I was involved in the other transfigurations as one-by-one they slipped away and winked into the night.

To say that I was overcome by all this is to simply lose the meanings of words. I was frozen to the bar stool, a lump of space-time matter attempting to assimilate the meaning of meaning, and I was still there at four o'clock when Souza and the advance guard entered the house.

Someone turned on the lights and someone else threw the main power breaker to the equipment. That broke my spell but I still sat there a frozen lump while Souza ventured into the circle.

A moment later, I heard him say, his voice coming as though from the far side of the universe, "They're dead. My God, they're all dead."

But I knew better. I could still see in the eye of my mind that thoroughly delighted and enraptured old face of my good friend Holden as he swirled to a kinder place, where time and age are not even states of mind, simply do not exist, and cannot be found in the meaning of meaning.

Ho! Bully!

EPILOGUE
Casefile Wrap-Up

Well, I did not get that ride in a saucer, or even see one, but any flying machine has to be satisfied with ranking as a minor phenomenon and nowhere in the same class with jinn, so what the hell. I guess they departed with the team, because I have found no "static" around Palomar since that event.

But where did they "depart" to? "Where *is* that?" as Holden would say.

I wish I knew. I have had all manner of weird dreams, almost on a daily basis, ever since—but they do not really tell me anything useful. It is not enough to simply declare that they are "dead," because I really cannot think of them that way. There were no marks on the bodies, no visible evidence of any sort of destructive violence, and I cannot believe that those people were even remotely thinking of "dying"—at least not in the usual sense in which we humans commonly think of death. Rather, they evinced all the excitement and sense of adventure of any travelers embarking on a delightful exploration of uncharted territory. The general mental atmosphere shared by that entire group during those final minutes on earth was one of "sober joy," if that is not a contradiction in terms.

I have to believe that they had some understanding, or at least some presentiment, of what they were headed toward. The whole phenomenon of biological age regression, mind-blowing in its own right, was reduced to a mere side-effect in their total sensing of what was opening to them. Certainly they had not invited me to join them in a "suicide pact," for God's sake, but in an exciting adventure.

And maybe they were not the first to experience something like this. Certainly our myths, legends, and religious beliefs—and these are legion—must be based on something more substantial than mere imagination. All the mystery religions have their equivalent of "the ascension" as well as various concepts of conscious union and personal relationships with the divine. Where such ideas have come from, barring divine revelation, is anybody's guess, so feel free to call it how you see it.

This group was not a religious group, unless you want to call science a religion—as well it may be. I believe that they regarded the jinn as a natural phenomenon and that they saw nothing at all supernatural about the circumstances—no more so than, say, had they been boarding a flying saucer for transport to another universe.

To this world, of course, they were indeed dead. The official "cause of death" was recorded as "radiation poisoning," but don't hold your breath waiting for evidence of that to be presented to a coroner's jury—or even for a jury, period. Also do not sit up waiting for any sort of public statement from Washington on this case, not if the eyes and jawlines of that Pentagon task force mean anything. They "debriefed" me for twelve hours straight then threw up their hands and ordered me to remain available for further "testimony," but I've heard nothing from them since the day I drove down off that mountain. The mountain is still there, of course, and that giant eye on the sky continues to probe the mysteries of the space-time universe.

Greg Souza is back into his routine with industrial security, on the surface, anyway, and he has yet to evince any curiosity whatever about the events of those final hours at Palomar. One scenario too many, maybe. For one of the lighter and almost comical sidelights to this case, Souza was actually "retained" by a group that sometimes fronts for the iron curtain diplomatic missions in this country. He'd also been "retained," of course, by our own government, so he was riding both steeds for awhile, there, trying to pull the ends together. I have heard nothing to this day about the operators I tangled with, their identities, none of it. It's as though none of it ever happened, except that final event, there, atop the mountain, and I guess that is just as well.

I did learn that none of these scientists left any immediate family. Isaac's estate, most of which was tied up in that mansion in Glendale, went to establish a fund for particularly gifted students who would be lost to science without financial assistance. The childless Summerfields, Holden and Laura, left just about everything to a trust that had been in place for years to be used "for the advancement and integration of the sciences, the arts, and the philosophies"—with a significant percentage of that directed toward Pala scholars.

I guess that about covers all the bases. But I do need to say a thing or two about that which occurred between the bases. This case, for me, began and ended with death. Those who cannot discern the qualitative distinction between the two modes of death exemplified here by Mary Ann Cunningham, on the one hand, and Holden Summerfield, say, on the other, will have found little meaning to this record and have probably wasted their time with it.

The difference, to me, and especially in the later reflections upon it, is both stunning and illuminating when viewed through the collective passions and paradoxes of mankind. Most every space-based religion, such as Judaism, Christianity, Moslem, Hindu, *et al*, have their analogs of "spirit" infusing matter to produce life on earth, the departure of that spirit into another reality as their explanation of death, and they all have their transfiguration stories in which this spirit is liberated from its entrapping matter through some direct, seemingly magical, agency. So I see no fundamental trespass, here, with most religious concepts—though I am sure there will be those who do.

In the same sense, the state of the physical sciences in this latter quarter of the twentieth century is such that the modern physicist is for all the world an alchemist and wizard, in constant touch with the abstracts of reality and daily lifting up the veils of existence to reveal a marvelously intricate and stunningly "smart" creation, yet none have physically touched the human mind, the instrument through which all understanding comes, nor has there been a productive grapple with the mysterious force that turns dumb matter to purposeful activity—so I see no fundamental trespass, here, with the speculative tenets of science, either, though—again—I am sure there will be those who do.

I need to say a word or two about Mary Ann Cunningham, since it was that unfortunate but coincidental death that propelled me into this case. I learned through a meeting with Souza and the L.A. police, a few days after I left Palomar, that Mary Ann had somehow discovered that Isaac was involved with fetus and embryo research, and she could not get out of her mind the possible connection with that and Isaac's role in her decision to abort her child. There was no connection, of course—hell, anyone interested in acquiring such specimens did not need to go out and recruit donors—but Mary Ann had voiced vague suspicions to co-workers at Griffith and seemed upset over the possibility that her "baby" was being kept alive in a test tube somewhere. The group had learned of all this and had dispatched Jennifer to Griffith to reassure Mary Ann and to explain the facts of fetal/embryo research. Jennifer, then, certainly had been among the last to see Mary Ann alive, because it was on that very day that Mary Ann's own life was senselessly and brutally aborted.

Her killer was apprehended, by the way, and the very thorough L.A. cops have it nailed. Several prominent criminal lawyers are right now vying for the limelight defense of this utterly indefensible serial killer—but what the hell, it's that kind of world, the one we've built for ourselves, so I guess we have to live with it. Perhaps that is not so important as what this killer has to die with—and what he will take with him to Holden's next crucible.

Why didn't I take that "trip" with the team? For the same reason that Mary Ann should not have been snatched away. I gave you, above, in the record of the case, a quotation from Vachel Lindsay given me by Holden. I looked up that poet, later, and I'd like to give you a few more lines from Lindsay, from *The Congo and Other Poems:*

> Let not young souls be
>   smothered out before
> They do quaint deeds and
>   fully flaunt their pride.

That is why I did not take the trip, I have not fully flaunted my pride, and that is why Mary Ann should not have died when she did and especially as she did. I did not think to ask Isaac whether his views on death had changed; you may recall the earlier record in which he is quoted as saying there is no such thing as a decent death. I am sure that he would amend that, now, and that he would regard his own "death" as the most "decent" act of his life. But, you see, Isaac had fully flaunted his pride, and he'd done many quaint deeds; in that context, death by any device could be regarded as a noble monument to an exhilarating adventure. In this particular context, "death" became a triumph.

Freud said that "the goal of all life is death" and spoke of a "death instinct"—but that does not define death, itself, and who among us can say what death truly is?

Henry Ward Beecher, on his deathbed, declared, "Now comes the mystery"—and Socrates, in his final summation, told his contemporaries, "And now the time has come when we must depart; I to my death, you to go on living. But which of us is going to the better fate is unknown to all except God."

I do not believe that the goal of life is death, not unless we find a new definition for death. The goal of life, as it has been evidenced in the play upon this planet, has been toward an ever-expanding expression of existence, the search for unfoldment, the sheer joy of experience. What we commonly perceive as death need not draw a curtain upon that play— except perhaps to set the stage for a new act and the progressive unfoldment of a brilliantly beautiful story.

Holden has not dropped in to visit, yet, not in any way that I could recognize, but I do have those moments when I feel that I am sharing a new perception with a very old friend who is delighted by the interchange; and, now and then, when I am looking at a sunrise or into a baby's eyes or at a magnificent work of art or watching lovers young and old with magic in their gazes, I find myself shouting to myself, "Ho! Bully!" It is a beautiful play, yes.

And that is where we are, you know, all of us.

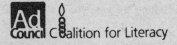